T0418109

HARDCASE

Center Point
Large Print

HARDCASE

MATT KINKAID

CENTER POINT LARGE PRINT
THORNDIKE, MAINE

This Center Point Large Print edition
is published in the year 2025 by arrangement with
Golden West Inc.

The text of this Large Print edition is unabridged.
In other aspects, this book may vary
from the original edition.
Printed in the United States of America
on permanent paper sourced using
environmentally responsible foresting methods.
Set in 16-point Times New Roman type.

ISBN: 979-8-89164-548-6

The Library of Congress has cataloged this record
under Library of Congress Control Number: 2025930451

PRINCIPAL CHARACTERS

JOHN PASCO
Lean, tough ex-convict. Lives only for revenge against the man who had him put into prison.

OTTO KELLER
One of the biggest ranchers on the Texas Panhandle. Hated and hunted by Pasco.

SILAS HORNSBY
Owner of the Crazy Creek spread and waging a cattle war with Keller.

MYRA
Keller's wife, who had loved Pasco, but loved power more.

CARL LEVI
The tough gunslinger who ramrods the Crazy Creek outfit.

Chapter One

They were finishing up the spring branding that day, and in a way John Pasco was sorry to see the work come to an end. It was hot, dirty work, and the air around the branding corral swirled with sticky red-clay dust that clung to your clothes, clotted your nostrils, mixed with the sweat on your face and ran in red rivulets all the way down your torso to the saddle-soaked seat of your pants. It wasn't easy work, but it was what John Pasco knew, and he enjoyed it.

He grinned now, listening to Charley Wilder's expert cursing, as the big man plunged his light little cutting horse into the bawling herd. The little bay charged with absolute fearlessness between two wild range cows, cut a calf away from its mother and herded it toward the branding fire.

John Pasco delighted in the mincing, dainty way the cutting horse lifted its hoofs, picking its way through the herd. He laughed outright as an old mossyhorn charged at the pony's flank and Charley Wilder let out a bellow of anger. Still cursing, Wilder twisted in the saddle and slammed the sharp toe of his boot at the cow's tender nose.

"Get this damned critter, Johnny!" he shouted. "I got me a war on my hands!"

7

Pasco already had the loop of his lariat shook out. The calf spurted forward in fright and John Pasco's roan mount shot after it. He waited until the precise moment, running the calf toward the fire. When the moment came he let go of the loop, watching it shoot straight ahead and settle around the critter's neck. The calf leaped almost straight up as Pasco snubbed his lariat to the saddlehorn. The roan squatted back, almost on its haunches, holding the lariat tight as John Pasco spilled out of the saddle and went down the rope to dump and tie the animal at the edge of the fire.

"Hell's afire!" The brander jumped away, snatching up the hot Bar-H-X branding iron. "What're you trying to do, Johnny, dump him right in the middle of my fire?"

The brander sounded angry, but John Pasco knew he was being handed a compliment. If there is anything a cowhand hates it's walking, even if it is only a few steps. The closer you can throw a calf to a brander's fire, the better he likes it.

"What do you want me to do?" Pasco demanded. "Brand him for you?"

They both grinned. The glowing iron was placed against the calf's side, hissing as the acrid smell of burning hair was added to the strangling dust.

"That does it," Charley Wilder said, riding up as they untied the bawling calf and let it go back to its mother.

They heard the hollow ringing of the dinner triangle, and slowly began to beat some of the dust from their clothes. Three more Bar-H-X riders joined them, leaving two men to take care of the loose herd, and they rode slowly, wearily, up the grade toward the main ranch buildings.

"By hell," Charley Wilder said, "I'll be glad when this job's over. I almost lost me a good cutting horse out there. Not to mention almost getting a pair of horns in my own gut."

"That would of been too bad," one of the riders said soberly. "Good cutting horses are hard to come by."

They laughed, turning their horses over to the wrangler, and headed toward the bunkhouse to wash up. They lined up at the long wash bench outside the bunkhouse, some of the men taking off their shirts and splashing cold well water over the upper half of their bodies. John Pasco left his shirt on, as he always did except at night when he was alone. He soaped his face and neck around his collarless shirt, lathered his hands and arms, and then rinsed off in the shockingly cold water.

"Today'll see the end of the branding," Charley Wilder said, splashing beside him. "Some of the hands are going in to Sandy Ford tonight and maybe celebrate a little."

"Maybe I'll join in," Pasco said, "if it's not a private party."

"It ain't. You know you've been invited plenty of times."

John Pasco dried off on a flour-sack towel taken from the stack at the end of the bench. He was thinking that Charley Wilder was the only man on the ranch that he could always feel comfortable with. He liked them all well enough; they were just ordinary cowhands on an ordinary ranch doing an ordinary job. They worked hard when there was a job to do, drank hard when there wasn't, fought hard at almost any time about almost anything. And Wilder, he thought, could outdrink and outwork and outfight any of them, excepting the foreman, but Charley didn't make a point of it. Maybe that was the thing that was different about him.

They went across the ranch yard to the cook shack, which was a lean-to shed against the side of the main ranch house. They ate in almost complete silence, as cowhands always do. Canned milk and bread and pitchers of hot coffee were passed wordlessly up and down the table. In five minutes the meal was over. They sat back chewing the last mouthful, grunting, belching, cursing the cook in a matter-of-fact way, from force of habit. No cook in his right mind would pay any attention to the cursing. It came with the job, like grease burns or other minor unpleasantries. And the cook knew the food was good—he served the same food in the ranch house.

Charley Wilder sat back picking his teeth, seeming to notice the empty place at the head of the table for the first time.

"Wonder where Bascom is?" he asked without much interest.

Bascom was the foreman on the Bar-H-X, a big, red-faced bulldog of a man with a reputation as a fighter, with guns as well as fists. He was quietly hated by his riders, but up until now no rider had taken it upon himself to do anything about it.

"I saw him go into the ranch house a while ago," Pasco said.

Wilder looked at him. "You mean to take his meal with the boss?"

"I don't know. I just saw him go in."

Big Wilder turned the prospect over in his mind ponderously. "Now that would be something to see," he decided. "I wonder why, though?"

"Maybe they're going to let somebody go," John Pasco said carefully. Already, not in his brain but deep in his belly, he began to realize that the end had come again. They were going to let somebody go, all right, and it was going to be him. A deep, aimless anger began to stir inside him. But it was an anger he could do nothing about.

"Now why would they do a thing like that?" Charley Wilder said, puzzled. "Hell, there's plenty of work to be done, even if the branding is over."

"Maybe I'm wrong," Pasco said. "We'll have to wait and see, I guess."

They didn't have to wait long. Bascom came out of the ranch house and around to the cook shack and jerked his head at Pasco. "Go over to the bunkhouse, Pasco," the foreman said abruptly. "The rest of you men get back to the branding corral and finish the job."

They got up unwillingly from the table, their dinnertime cut short. John Pasco could feel them looking at him curiously, wondering what Bascom had in store for him. They began to drift off toward the holding corral, where the wrangler was cutting out fresh horses for them. All of them but Charley Wilder.

"Why, hell!" the big man exploded, "it can't be *you,* if somebody's laid off. You're the best man they got in this outfit."

Pasco forced a grin. But he knew, and the others knew, that when a man was called to the bunkhouse in the middle of the day it meant the boss wanted to talk to him. "You better go on," he said, "before Bascom busts his girth. I'll see you after a while."

It was cool in the bunkhouse—as cool as it was anywhere in that Texas brush country, in June. John Pasco sat on his bunk, rolled another cigarette and waited. The bunkhouse was a long, boxlike affair with windows on both sides and at one end. The door was at the other end. There

12

were eight bunks in the place, and not much else. It was naked and bare and lonely. But for almost a year it had been John Pasco's home.

As he waited for Albert C. Crestwood, the owner of the Bar-H-X, John Pasco began to get his things together. There wasn't much to bother with in the way of clothing. Everything he had he could easily get into a blanket roll. He had three shirts, three pairs of faded cotton pants, and his anger. That was about all.

He did have a good horse, though, and a good saddle. He had scrupulously saved his money to buy them, and he was glad of that. And he had a good pair of boots—bench-made boots that he'd had made especially for himself in the best leather shop in Sandy Ford. And he owned a black hat; not the wide-brimmed plainsman's hat, but a narrow-brimmed, peak-crowned hat peculiar to cowhands in the brush country of southwest Texas, and nowhere else that he knew of.

He also had a Colt .45 caliber single-action revolver. He had almost forgotten about that— but not quite. It was the first thing he had bought, on his first payday, after coming out of Huntsville.

He got the revolver out of the bottom of his warbag, took the oiled cloth from around it and held it carefully in the palm of his hand. It was a beautiful thing, created by loving hands of the toughest steel, and its single reason for being was to kill.

That was the reason John Pasco had bought it. To kill a man.

He began to think about it coolly, leaving emotion out of it. It's clear, he thought, that I can't go on like this. It'll be the same anywhere I go. Sooner or later they'll find out.

Carefully, he wiped the excess oil from the revolver. He punched out the five cartridges in the cylinder, wiped them clean with the oiled rag, and replaced them. It was a good gun. He balanced it delicately in one hand and then the other, thinking back to the day he had bought it. He had bought the gun and the cartridges and went out on the range and practiced for half a day, to make sure he hadn't lost his touch. He had shot a dozen milk cans to pieces, he remembered, at a distance of thirty paces. He hadn't lost any-thing—not in the way of shooting.

That had been two years and three jobs ago, he thought now, buckling on his cartridge belt and slipping the .45 into the stiff leather holster. And he still hadn't killed his man—not yet.

He couldn't say just why he hadn't gone ahead and done it, the way he had planned through those long, sleepless nights in Huntsville Prison. It wasn't because the man didn't need killing. Any man who would deliberately lie another

14

man into three years of prison needed killing.

John Pasco heard the sound of boots on the packed clay earth outside the bunkhouse. The door opened and Albert Crestwood came in, followed by the foreman.

Crestwood was a slight, greying little man who ran the Bar-H-X from a tilt-back chair inside the ranch house most of the time. Occasionally, when there were major decisions to be made, he would come out and mix with the riders. But not often. As was the case with many big Texas outfits, the foreman was the one who actually ran the ranch.

"Pasco," the owner said mildly, "my foreman tells me that the branding is about over."

"That's right," John Pasco said. "Today'll see the end of it." But he was thinking, why the hell doesn't he come out and say what's on his mind? Why do they always have to beat around the bush?

"I hate to do this, Pasco," Crestwood said, the words coming faster now, as though he were anxious to get it over with. "You're one of our best riders, and I was telling Bascom that just the other day. But you know there's always a slack season after branding—"

His voice ran down like a clock with a weak spring, and Bascom stepped in. "What the boss means," he said finally, "is we got to let somebody go. It's going to be you, Pasco."

There didn't seem to be anything to say to that, so John Pasco remained silent.

"Maybe in the fall," Crestwood said vaguely, "maybe we'll be hiring again then, if you're around—"

"But I doubt it," Bascom the foreman put in bluntly.

Crestwood looked hurt at the foreman's crudeness, but he didn't deny what Bascom had said. Nervously, he got a cigar from his vest pocket and rolled it on his tongue. He noticed Pasco's .45 then, and decided he didn't like it. "Of course," he said, "you'll draw a full month's pay. Bascom will take care of that."

"All right," John Pasco said woodenly.

"Like I said, maybe in the fall—"

Pasco stood up abruptly. "I said it was all right," he said in sudden anger. "What do you want me to do? Lick your boots and beg for the job back? I'm being fired—let's let it go at that."

The ranch owner was shaken at the sudden outburst of anger. He took two steps back, uncertainly. "Bascom," he said, wiping his sweaty forehead, "you'd better pay him off." He turned stiffly and marched the length of the bunkhouse and went out the door.

Bascom grinned. "Now that wasn't smart," he said dryly. "If you had talked right, maybe you could have gone on working for us."

The quick anger had burned itself out. John Pasco sat down again, looking at the foreman, thinking to himself that Bascom was a better man

16

than Crestwood. At least, if Bascom had had his way, he would have fired him honestly, and not beat around the bush about it. "That's a lie," he said calmly, beginning to roll a cigarette. "I'll never work for the Bar-H-X again, nor for any other outfit in this part of Texas."

Bascom chuckled quietly as he counted out forty dollars and threw it on Pasco's bunk. "There's your pay."

Pasco looked at the money but didn't touch it. "How did Crestwood find out?" he asked. "Did you tell him?"

"About the spell you put in at Huntsville? Sure." The foreman grinned. "I saw you washing the other night—with your shirt off."

John Pasco nodded, thinking vaguely that he should hate the foreman, and wondering why he didn't.

"It's nothing personal," the foreman said. "We just don't hire convicts."

"To keep you straight," Pasco said, "I'm not a convict any more. They let me out two years ago."

The foreman sat down on a half-made bunk, still grinning amiably. "That's what you say. But look at my side of it. How do I know what trouble you've been in, or are maybe going to get in?" He glanced at the .45. "You have to be careful about who you hire on a ranch—there's nothin' to keep a rider from driving half our herd across

17

the Border and selling to the Mexicans, if he was that kind. Hell, I don't even know if Pasco's your real name."

"I'm not asking for my job back."

They sat quietly for a while. The foreman wasn't grinning now. "You got it pretty bad," he said finally. "Worse than the others I've seen."

"I hit a prison guard my first week there."

"Now that was a fool thing to do."

"I was mad," John Pasco said. "Half crazy, I guess. I still wasn't used to the idea that a man could be sent to prison for something he didn't do."

The foreman sat there for a long moment, looking at him. "If you want to talk about it, I'll listen."

John Pasco had half a mind to tell him, just to see if he could rid himself of some of the hate and anger by talking. But instead he began throwing his clothes on the blanket to make the roll. Bascom sighed and got up to go.

"I'll have your horse fed on grain," he said at the door. "Drop by the cook shack when you get ready to leave and I'll get the biscuit-shooter to give you a grub sack."

Pasco looked up, puzzled by the fact that he had known Bascom for almost a year and had never seen this side of him.

"Thanks."

He heard the screen door slam. Pasco rolled the

blanket with his clothes inside it, then wrapped his poncho around it and tied it. There was nothing more to do, except to get saddled and ride. Still he waited in the empty bunkhouse, tying and re-tying the blanket roll, thinking of aimless things to do to keep him there a while longer.

He realized that he was waiting for big Charley Wilder, his friend, to come and say good-by. After more time had passed he realized that Wilder wasn't coming. None of them would come. Word had already got around that he was a hardcase convict, or a hardcase ex-convict. They didn't want anything to do with him.

He felt himself smiling grimly. You never knew what a man was really like . . .

Disgustedly, he slung the blanket roll over his shoulder and headed toward the corral, where his roan horse was. There was a difference, he thought, between men who had been to prison and hardcases. There were plenty of cowpunchers who had spent time in Huntsville for one reason or another, and when they came out they were about the same as they had been when they went in. They took their punishment philosophically, even laughed about it, and they went back for their old jobs and their old bosses hired them on again.

A hardcase was different. He fought like a wild king stallion that refused to be broken. His eyes became slitted and quick from the endless nights of the dungeon, like the eyes of a cat. And his back bore the mark of the whip—the lean, hard whip that struck with the ferocity of a bullet, that tore and ripped and laid open the flesh.

Thinking of it made John Pasco aware of his own back. The badge of the hardcase. The unbroken stallion that had been trained by the whip to kill. It had gone as far as it could go, he thought. He had put it off for two years, hoping that somehow the bitterness and anger would wear itself out. But it had only seemed to get worse. For a while—as it had been on the Bar-H-X —everything had been fine. He had a job he liked, friends, money every payday. But every time it came to an end, the way it had this time. They didn't want hardcases. They were afraid of them. And they wouldn't let you be anything else if you had the mark, the way John Pasco had.

On the way to the barn he stopped at the saddle shed to pick up his rig. There he shouldered the thirty-odd pounds of leather and wood that he was so proud of and which had cost him almost six full months' pay and hard ranch work. There was also a pair of battered leather chaps, but he decided that he wouldn't need them if he was leaving the brush country. He didn't need the dangling *tapaderos* on his stirrups either, for that matter, but he let them stay because he had become accustomed to them.

Bascom wasn't in the barn. The roan had been taken out of the corral and put into a stall with a troughful of corn. Pasco slapped the horse on the rump as he threw up the blanket and saddle. Eat all you can hold, he thought. It's apt to be the last corn you'll see for a while.

He lingered in the barn for several minutes, waiting for the horse to finish eating. He could hear the noise of the riders down by the branding corral, and smoldering anger flared up again within him. He knew that he was a better ranch hand than any of them, but that only added to his bitterness.

But he couldn't blame them. How could they know what was going through a man's mind? They knew that horses that refused to be broken became killers, and men were not so very different from horses, in a lot of ways.

Bascom was not at the cook shack, either, when Pasco rode by to pick up the grub sack. Well, he thought wryly, what did you want in the way of a send-off, anyway? A brass band? He took the grub sack from the cook—coffee, bacon, cornmeal, salt, and a few pieces of cooked cornbread—and lashed it on behind the saddle with his roll.

He rode across a rough, brush-tangled draw and saw Bascom sitting a little paint horse up on a rocky ridge. He sat as solidly as a stone statue, a strange, outlandish figure thrown against the

21

brilliant blue sky. He reined his mount around, grinning slightly as John Pasco rode up the slope.

"I see the cook got you fixed up," he said.

"I could have rode off with the whole damned cook shack," John Pasco said without humor. "It seems like I got myself quite a reputation as a hardcase, for some reason. I couldn't have got more service if I had been the whole Bass gang."

The foreman laughed an ugly, dry laugh that Pasco had hated for almost a year but now liked, for some reason that he couldn't understand.

"Maybe you can tell me," Pasco said, "why they're all of a sudden afraid of me. It's more than I can figure out."

"It's more than fear, although that has something to do with it, I guess." The foreman looked at Pasco and then turned his eyes away. "You're different, for one thing. Even if they can't see those whip scars on your back, they know they're there, and that makes you different from them. A renegade, kind of."

"Whip scars don't change a man," John Pasco said angrily. "I've seen men take beatings harder and more often than I did, and people don't look at them the way they look at me. Even when they saw the scars."

"That's just the trouble," the foreman grinned. "The whippings didn't change you. I guess the men sense that, and it makes them realize what gutless animals they really are, and that's the reason they don't want you around. Now if they'd broken you, things would be different. You'd have more friends than you'd know what to do with, because most men know inside their small souls that they themselves would have broken. A few trips to the dungeon, a few trips to the whipping rack, and they would have been crawling gobs of gutless jelly. And they know it. You're not ever going to have many friends, Pasco, and you might as well get used to it."

It was the longest speech John Pasco had ever heard the foreman make.

Abruptly, Bascom laughed that ugly laugh again. "Why," he said, "you could get your job back right now, I'll bet, if you wanted to. All you'd have to do is come crawling back to Crestwood with your tail between your legs, and he would hire you on. Probably as a top-hand."

"To hell with Crestwood. And the Bar-H-X, and all the rest of it."

"That's what I thought," Bascom said, laughing. "I wouldn't want to be in your boots, Pasco."

"Why? You're one of the most hated men in this part of Texas. Are you so much better off than I am?"

"Sure," the foreman said. "I'm twice the man of anybody on the ranch, and they all know it. But I don't have the proof on my back, the way you do."

"Is that the reason you had me fired?" Pasco

asked bluntly. "Because you were afraid I was a better man than you were?"

"Maybe. Yes, that was part of it, but the important thing was that it never would have worked out anyway. You would only have caused trouble, and in the end you would have to go off and kill the man who lied you into prison, anyway. Are you good with that forty-five?"

"I manage to stay alive," John Pasco said tightly.

The foreman nodded again. "You'll need more than a gun to keep you alive when you start squaring things up. But go ahead and do it your own way. That's the real reason I fired you, I guess."

"Who said I was going to kill anybody?" he demanded.

The foreman shrugged, as though he had run out of anything to say. He stood up in his stirrups, spotting a range cow down in the draw below. "Good luck, Pasco," he said, reining his pony around. "You'll need it."

Chapter Two

During the next few days John Pasco spent a lot of time thinking about the Bar-H-X foreman. He had to admit that Bascom was a tough, honest man—probably the only honest man with the outfit—and one of his phrases got lodged in the back of Pasco's mind, and he couldn't get it out. *You could get your job back, if you wanted to.*

There was nothing he wanted more than to go back to the routine of hard work and sweat, and put the past out of his mind. It was the kind of hard, tough life that he was made for and had been trained for. But in the middle of thinking about it, he would remember the whip, and the dungeon, and the prison, and anger would well up and almost choke him.

He wondered if Bascom had been right. "In the end you would have to go back and kill the man who lied you into prison," he had said.

At last he forgot about Bascom and thought of other things. There was Messina, he thought. Think about Messina, and the Muleshoe-P, and long-ago times. You can even think about *her,* he thought, because all that was long ago and it doesn't make any difference now. . . .

The Muleshoe-P, of course, was his ranch, or rather, had been his ranch. It got its name from the little creek that crawled along the southern boundary of his land and suddenly bending to form an inverted U. The brand was a U with a big block P for Pasco in the center, and it was registered and had a place in the Brand Book right alongside such famous brands as the Double-O-Star and the Crazy Creek and the Rocker-O and all the others.

He had been proud of his brand, and of the ranch too, although it was just a little place— what they called a cockleburr ranch, or a haywire outfit—up in Messina County, in the Texas Panhandle. The Muleshoe-P ran less than fifty head of cattle, while outfits like the Crazy Creek ran five thousand head and thought nothing of it. It was big country up there, and the ranchers were big men. Almost two years went by before anybody realized that there was such an outfit as the Muleshoe-P.

That was his ranch, a one-room stockade house, a barn, three pole and rawhide corrals, and all of northwest Texas to graze in because it was open range and all the cattlemen were using it.

He got his start, like most of the big ranchers got theirs, by mavericking. In the brush country it was called brushpopping, and up north it was mavericking, but it amounted to the same thing. You went out on a horse, or on foot if you didn't have a horse, and you searched the gullies and draws of the back country, and when you came upon a calf with no brand and no mother to tell you whom it belonged to, then you burned the maverick with your own brand. There was no law against it.

Messina was the county seat of Messina County, about five miles south of the Muleshoe-P, where most of the cattlemen made their headquarters. It was a quiet, small town, weathered with many blazing summers and whiplash winters. To live there, a man had to run the chance of freezing, or, a few months later, dropping dead from a heat stroke. It wasn't an easy place for men, but the grass was good and cattle thrived, and those were the things that counted to a man who wanted to be a rancher.

But, he thought, that was long ago. It's been five years since I've even seen the place. Three of those years were spent in prison.

He fought his bitterness down and, with effort, held his anger in check.

Pasco took out his .45 and began cleaning it absently by the light of his fire. As he worked methodically, carefully, his mind kept going back. Where did it begin? he wondered. He knew how it would end.

Had it begun with the war? Maybe. His pa had been killed while fighting with Hood's Texans in some far-off place called Virginia and for a cause which had been passionate at the time but which was now blurred with years and seemed neither important nor real. His ma had died in the summer of '72, along with many others, when the milk-fever epidemic swept over that part of the country. John Pasco was fifteen at the time, and he had been on his own since then.

It was a time when the cattleman was beginning to ascend the king's throne in Texas. The Easterners were starving for beef, they said, and would pay as high as twenty-five dollars a head for four-year-olds. Texas was overrun with beef, most of it unbranded range cows dropped during the war years; longhorned beasts as wild as the country itself, as dangerous as tigers.

The strong men, the hungry men of Texas, began beating trails through the wilderness of Indian Territory. Powerful ranches and cattle companies were formed almost overnight as they staged country-wide roundups to gather the unbranded beef. It was work for big men, strong men who could grasp and hold an idea that was new and powerful. The few men who were big enough and strong enough—Croy Hilderbrand, Jules and Otto Keller, Silas Hornsby—had grown and prospered. But John Pasco had been just a kid then.

And he hadn't been very smart, either, he thought now. A smart kid never would have started his spread up north on the Muleshoe, where the water was plentiful and the grass was thick, for that was Otto Keller's range—

the Keller Kingdom, they called it—where his Rocker-O cattle roamed the valleys of belly-deep buffalo grass. Three big outfits held that country in an iron grip, making a joke of the free-range law—Keller's Rocker-O, Silas Hornsby's Crazy Creek brand, and Croy Hilderbrand's Double-O Star.

John Pasco laughed without humor. No, he hadn't been smart. A smart kid would have staked out in the southern half of the county and starved slowly to death, along with the other small haywire ranchers and squatters and sod-busters. He would never have made a go of it there because the grass was skimpy and there was no water at all, except for a few mudholes in the spring of the year. But that south-county land had one good thing about it—it was so poor that you didn't have to worry about the big ranchers moving in on you.

Of course, there had been more of it than the simple business of mavericking on land that Otto and his father, old Jules, claimed as their own. Maybe, Pasco thought now, if it hadn't been for Myra, none of the trouble would have happened.

Closing his eyes, he could see her just the way she had looked that day more than five years ago, and he wondered if she had changed.

He didn't think she had—not Myra. Then his mind went back again, remembering the first meeting between them.

• • •

John Pasco remembered how awkward he had been, and how he had gawked and mumbled, feeling the heat rushing to his face; and even now he wasn't sure if it was her beauty that had struck him with such awe, or if it was simply because she was the daughter of Croy Hilderbrand.

Croy Hilderbrand's Double-O Star was already the biggest ranch in northwest Texas, and one of the biggest in the state. The rancher and his family lived in a big two-story frame house where the Muleshoe forked with Crazy Creek, and John Pasco had heard people say that the family ate their meals from china imported all the way from England, as thin and as delicate as egg shells.

Occasionally, though not often, Hilderbrand and his wife—who had been a beauty in her day, people said—and Myra would come into Messina. Pasco had never seen Mrs. Hilderbrand or Myra in any Messina store other than Peg Manning's "Ladies' Wear Emporium," as she called it. Mrs. Hilderbrand was a great lady back in Virginia, before the war. She didn't mix with the people of Messina. And neither did Myra.

Old Hilderbrand was a big, rough-featured bull of a man who seemed eternally amazed that he should have such a wife and daughter. He'd won what he had with his gun and his fists and a steel-trap brain. His ambition, as everybody knew, was to have the whole of the Texas Panhandle as his personal grazing ground—but he was getting old. And Keller and Hornsby were standing in his way.

In those days John Pasco worked wherever he could, as stableboy, or blacksmith's helper. And he nursed a small dream. Some day he wanted a little place of his own, a place where there was enough grass and water to work his own brand. Others had done it. It wasn't impossible.

After a long while of working and saving, he had enough money to pay for a runted little brush pony and a second-hand saddle, and that was all he needed to start mavericking. He started on the bend of the Muleshoe and worked to the west mostly, keeping scrupulously away from the Rocker-O herds, wanting no trouble. Whenever he had a minute to spare from his cowhunting, he worked on his corrals and sheds and the little one-room shack to live in. Thinking back, John Pasco guessed he was completely happy in those days; as happy as work and a taste of success can make a man.

But his mind kept going back to Myra as he lay there on the bank of the nameless creek, his brush fire dying, the stars very cold and very aloof.

She had almost run him down, he remembered. John had been cutting cottonwood saplings along the creek bank when that big black gelding of hers came plunging through a plum thicket, looking as big as a railroad locomotive as it came crashing down on him. She was a very good rider, her skirts swirling, her eyes bright with sudden excitement, as she had reined the horse over barely enough to miss him. She had been laughing all the time, and that was when she had spoken whatever those first words had been.

Pasco had thrown himself on his face, toward the creek bank. He'd got up angrily, thinking, nobody but a damned fool woman would punish a horse like that! Forgetting, for the moment, about himself. . . .

Then he really saw her for the first time, and realized who she was. And that was when the awkwardness seized him, and his tongue seemed to get stuck to the roof of his mouth. She must have looked much the same as her mother had looked many years before; as straight as an arrow, a haughty tilt to her blonde head, a flash to her eyes. It was her laughter, though, that John Pasco remembered in particular; it was clear and ringing, the way laughter should be in that wide country. After a moment she noticed the corral he was building, a hundred yards or so up the grassy slope from the creek.

She said, "You must ride for the Rocker-O. Are Jules and Otto building a line camp down here?"

He mumbled that it was his own camp he was building.

Her eyebrows went up at that, and the laughter went out of her voice. "Do you mean," she asked, as though she didn't believe him, "that you're nesting on Rocker-O range?"

"It's free range," he corrected. "And I'm not nesting."

The words trailed off. Her lips were very red, he thought, and her skin looked as smooth as waxed ivory. Those things, in a country where everything became faded and rough from the weather, were startling.

"Well—" she said, and she didn't seem to know just what to say. "Does Otto Keller, or his father, know you're down here?"

"I guess not."

"They have cattle down here," she said. "I saw a bunch just a few minutes ago."

"Sure," he said, admiring the way her hair shone whenever the sun struck it. "I don't bother them, though. They can cut my herd any time they feel like it."

She looked at him in a strange sort of way, half frowning, but still looking amused. Then abruptly she laughed again, reining the big gelding around. "You don't have to worry about my telling them," she said. "I'll keep your secret for you." She cracked the black's rump with a short quirt, and the big animal exploded into a run. As John Pasco stood watching, they disappeared behind a cluster of willows and brush.

Forget her, he told himself. She's not for the likes of you, John Pasco.

Maybe if it hadn't been for the Kellers, he'd never have seen her again. He remembered back now with fresh bitterness to the day of his first meeting with Otto and Jules—a hot day, he recalled, and he had just returned from a two-day hunt in the hills. He was washing in the creek when he first saw the riders, four of them, top the grassy rise to the north.

He had expected this encounter, half dreading and half welcoming it—dreading it because the power of the Kellers was legend in the country of north Texas, welcoming it because he knew he was within his rights and he'd be glad to get the thing settled. He walked toward his shack, noticing that it was poorly built and already beginning to sag.

Old Jules Keller, red-faced, bearded, bulging and heavy with hard fat, rode in the van of the party. Otto, exactly the man his father had been thirty years before, rode to the left and slightly behind the old man, in an almost military acceptance of authority. John Pasco waited in front of his shack, uncomfortable but not afraid, as they came ponderously toward him. I've got my rights, he kept thinking, and that knowledge kept him from flinching as the old man reined up directly in front of him and stared down at him with ill-controlled anger.

Jules Keller's naturally thick mouth was pulled thin as he glanced about at the poor buildings. He

34

spat suddenly, streaming tobacco juice into the powdery dust at John Pasco's feet. He spoke four words, harshly.

"Get off my land!"

Pasco's first impulse was to shrink back. The impulse passed almost instantly and anger took its place. He glanced quickly at Otto Keller, a thickset man who sat his horse solidly as a rock. He wore saddle-sweated blue serge pants, the frayed bottoms pushed carelessly into the tops of his work-battered boots. He wore a collarless hickory shirt, like any ranch hand, with salt stains under the armpits, and a loose-fitting serge vest culled from some long-discarded suit, stained with the spillings of a thousand forgotten meals. It was almost impossible to believe that this man—and his father, who looked no better— could be two of the most powerful men in Texas.

"You hear me?" Jules said angrily. "When I tell a man to get off my land, he gets off."

Pasco said, "It's not your land. It's free range, and I guess I've got as much right here as the next one."

The old man pulled back as though he had been slapped. For the first time Otto acted as if he had a mind of his own. He shifted in the saddle, almost lazily, grunting to his two riders. As Otto swung down, they swung down. I should have worn my gun, Pasco thought. The two riders rushed him and wrestled him to the ground.

"Stand him up," Otto said calmly.

Almost immediately he was jerked to his feet by the two riders, his hands held behind him.

"You going to get off our land?" Otto Keller asked.

"Like hell," Pasco shouted at him, and the words were hardly out of his mouth when Otto hit him in the face. The blow stunned Pasco. The shock, the pain buckled his knees and he lurched forward, held upright only by the efforts of the grunting riders. A sudden fury gave him strength to struggle for a moment, but even then he knew he didn't have a chance. The realization that the Kellers were too big for him, that he would lose his ranch before it was started, made him sicker than the pain. Otto hit him again, swinging his powerful shoulders, shifting his feet, shooting his enormous fist in like a pile driver. Pasco heard himself yelling and the yell was cut off abruptly with another blow to his ribs. Blackness seemed to open in front of him, and a great sickness.

Otto shot that hammerlike fist in again and again, but John Pasco was beyond pain. He felt only a great jarring shock as the blows landed. In that last moment he started to stare with a kind of morbid fascination as the fist rushed toward him. He thought, amazed, it's just a job of work for Otto. There's no expression at all on his face. Then the blackness opened wider and he fell into it.

It must have been a long time before he regained consciousness. His first awareness was of the smell of smoke. It drifted in white shredded ribbons across the ground, and he lay dumbly, wondering where the smoke was coming from. And finally the pain and soreness and throbbing reached his brain. Some ribs must be broken, he thought aimlessly, when he failed in an effort to raise himself to his hands and knees.

He lay for a long while, his eyes closed, for he realized now where the smoke was coming from. His corrals, his sheds, his shack were all burning. He kept his eyes closed because he didn't want to see it. . . .

He managed to crawl to the dugout—a small storm cellar affair that he had made when first coming to the Muleshoe—a dank-smelling, dirt-wall and dirt-floor place, merely a hole dug in the ground, with a roof of cottonwood branches laid across and more dirt piled on top of them. It was the kind of place nesters usually built, and he hated it and had built the shack as soon as possible.

But the dugout was all he had left. It was the only thing they couldn't burn.

He lay on the floor, breathing very carefully and shallowly, but even so his lungs felt full of fire. The slightest movement brought on new pain. He remained motionless, trying not to think.

They whipped me, he thought. It wasn't even a fight.

He had no way of knowing how long he lay there. He slept and it was night when he awoke, but he didn't know if it was the same night or a week later. It seemed like a lifetime, and he still couldn't move without rousing the needle-sharp pain in his side. His ribs should be bound tight, he knew, to bring the splintered ends together and keep them from puncturing something inside. Once he had seen a bronc peeler thrown; the man's lung had been punctured by a broken rib and bright red frothy blood had bubbled from his mouth.

He slept again, and then awoke. Dazzling sunlight streamed down the narrow shaft that served as the dugout's front door.

Slowly the facts began to come to him and he began to organize his anger. I'm not going to let them whip me like this, he thought soberly. I'll fight them. I don't care if it's the Kellers and the Hornsbys and the Hilderbrands all together; I'm not going to take this without fighting.

Then he forced himself to his hands and knees, and then to his feet, and he began stumbling up the dirt steps of the dugout. He made his way out into the sunlight and stood there swaying, blinking, sweat forming on his neck and running in cold little rivulets down his back.

That was when he heard the sound that he had waited so long for. But now he listened to the quick syncopated beat of hoofs far down the

38

creek, and it didn't mean a thing. When the big gelding nosed into view, following a bend in the creek, John Pasco stared blankly, and almost a full minute passed before he realized the rider was Myra Hilderbrand.

There was no flash of laughter in her eyes this time as she reined up sharply beside the charred poles that had once been a corral. She said flatly: "I see Otto and Jules found you."

"Yes," he said.

"Are you hurt? Other than your face, I mean."

He shook his head vaguely, still not sure that she was really there. "I don't know. My ribs, I think."

She slipped down from the sidesaddle in one flowing motion, landing lightly on her feet in the dust. She looped her reins loosely around a burned stump and came toward him.

"You'd better take off your shirt," she said briskly.

She acts as though she does this sort of thing every day, John Pasco thought. Maybe she follows after Otto and Jules, patching up what they break. But he began unbuttoning his shirt clumsily, and after a moment she said impatiently, "Let me do it."

Her hands were expert and quick. She opened his shirt and pulled it away from his shoulders and down his arms, as professionally as a nurse. Then she put her hands on either side of his rib cage and pressed in. A thin sliver of pain seemed to go through his skull, he felt the blood draining from his face.

"It's your ribs, all right," she said. "Turn around."

John Pasco wondered why she bothered. Her face seemed completely emotionless. Did she feel sorry for him? Did she feel more than that? But that was ridiculous. Croy Hilderbrand's daughter?

He turned around and then he heard the rustle of her skirts and the tearing of material.

"All right," she said, "you can turn back now."

While his back was turned she had taken off one of her petticoats and was now ripping it into narrow strips.

"Exhale," she said.

Pasco let the air go out of his lungs. With those sure, strong hands she bound the cloth around his chest so tightly that he could hardly breathe. But the ragged saw-tooth edge was gone from the pain.

"I don't know how good a job it is," she said. "You'd better see a doctor when you get to Messina."

He said, "I won't be going back soon."

Her eyebrows went up. "You can't stay here," she said evenly. "The Kellers will kill you; make no mistake about that."

"Then they'll have to do better than they did the last time."

For a moment her face was completely blank. Then suddenly she laughed. "You really mean it, don't you? You mean to stay right here."

She'll never be more beautiful than she is right now, John Pasco thought. He had an insane notion to reach out and touch her, to see if her skin was really as smooth as it looked. . . .

Chapter Three

He was a long way from the Muleshoe now. A long way from the Southwest brush country, too, as he slept on the bank of the forgotten creek.

Toward daybreak he must have dozed, for the sun was shooting brilliant yellow darts through the cottonwoods when he awakened. He got up sluggishly, his neck stiff from sleeping on the saddle, and went down to the stream to wash his face. His horse grazed idly up the creek, about a hundred yards away.

He built up the brush fire again and began preparing his breakfast. With his pocket knife he cut two thick slices from the slab of salt pork. While the meat was cooking, he mixed cornmeal and salt in a little water, patted the mixture into small cakes and put them in the pan to cook in the sizzling fat. Finally, after putting the hoecake and fatback to one side, he poured water into the skillet, added a handful of coffee, beginning to eat as he waited for the coffee to boil.

He began riding again as soon as he finished the grease-coated coffee, putting the brush country farther behind him. I'm getting closer, he thought. Every minute is putting me closer to Messina, closer to Otto Keller.

They'll hang you, a voice said. As sure as

there's a fire in hell, they'll hang you if you go gunning for him. It's not too late to turn back.

I've been turning back for two years, Pasco thought grimly. I'm through turning back.

Slowly, subtly, the country began to change as the days dragged one into another. John Pasco rode deeper and deeper into the monotonous wastes of the *Llano Estacado*, across the far western reaches of Red River, and at last he knew that Indian Territory would be on his right and Jess Chisum's cattle trail would be somewhere on the left, a long way off. He could look to the north and see what used to be Comanche country. It was Panhandle country; he could smell it, almost taste it in the air, and for a moment a surge of anticipation went through him, and he thought: I'm coming home!

Myra's laughter came faintly across the prairie now, as he rode with single-mindedness, always to the north. We were very young then, he thought heavily. It never would have worked anyway.

She had come back the next day—back to his burned-out place on the Muleshoe—and that surprised look had been in her eyes, as though she hadn't really expected to find him there.

"Don't you want to go on living?" she had asked abruptly.

"Sure," he said slowly. "But not like a dog to

be kicked by anybody that comes by and feels like swinging a boot."

"But you can't fight the Rocker-O!" she said, almost in anger.

"I guess I can't do anything else now."

She made an exasperated sound, still sitting on the black gelding like a queen. "You men make . . ." Shaking her head, the words trailed off. "Don't you understand? Otto Keller won't allow anybody on this land. He'll kill you, if he has to."

His anger had turned cold inside him and he was determined not to move.

"My father would do the same thing," she said, "if it was his land."

"It's nobody's land," he said stubbornly. "It's free range."

She rode away, disgusted with his stupidity, without saying another word.

John Pasco expected the worst. But at least he had a gun, and would use it if he had to. Three days passed. It was almost unbelievable that the Kellers hadn't come for the show-down.

He didn't guess the real reason until Myra came back again. John Pasco was working on his feed shed when he heard the syncopated catch of hoofs down by the creek.

"You're still here," she said, with no surprise in her voice this time.

"Yes," he mumbled, feeling the awkwardness creeping through him.

Her eyes looked tired. "You'll be all right for a while. How long, though, I don't know."

And for the first time he began to suspect that she must have intervened in his behalf. The idea was incredible—why should Croy Hilderbrand's daughter bother herself with a nobody, a mavericker?

He kicked dust with the toe of his boot, like an embarrassed schoolboy. Then he blurted, "Why did you do it?"

"Do what?" she asked innocently.

"I don't know how you managed it, but you stopped the Kellers from coming back here." A kind of helpless, unreasonable anger had taken hold of him. A man had to fight his own battles.

For a long moment she said nothing. Then she slipped out of the saddle and stood facing him, her eyes flashing. "They would have killed you!" she said tightly. "I would have done the same thing for a range calf, because a range calf doesn't have sense enough to take care of itself. And neither do you! You let yourself be beaten because of your pride; you'd even let yourself be killed because of it."

Then she turned and walked quickly away. Down by the creek, she paused under a tall rattling cottonwood, straight and rigid in her anger. After an uncertain moment, John Pasco

45

went down and stood beside her and grasped her shoulders.

"Why did you do it?" he heard himself demanding.

"Let me alone!" But she made no move to free herself.

"I have a right to know. It was my fight, not yours."

He never understood just how it happened. One moment he was grasping her shoulders, blurting questions, and the next moment she was in his arms. This is crazy, he remembered thinking. Old Hilderbrand will kill me sure, if the Kellers don't beat him to it! But the thought drifted off and was lost in this new wonder. Then he kissed her.

It was the first time a thing like that had ever happened to him, it was the first time he had ever held a girl in his arms, feeling the coolness of her mouth against his. His awkwardness seemed to disappear, and confidence and self-assurance took its place.

"Now do you know why?" she said quietly. "Do I have to tell you I love you?"

John Pasco felt that nothing would ever shock or surprise him again. He knew he loved her— had loved her since that first day when she had almost run him down with that big black.

"I guess," he said soberly, "I feel the same way."

"Is that the best you can do?"

She was teasing him now, but he didn't mind. "No," he said. "I love you."

Later, thinking back on it, he could almost believe that it had all been some kind of a strange dream, almost as though a spell had been cast upon him for a few minutes, and none of it had actually happened at all. He found himself moving dazedly through the ruins of his camp, searching out the wide hoofprints of the gelding in order to convince himself that she had really been there.

Then the obvious answer leaped into his mind. She's just teasing me, he thought. It's just a game for her, something to amuse herself with until something better comes along. But he didn't believe it.

She couldn't manage it often, for his place on the Muleshoe was a long ride from her father's headquarters to the east, but she did come back whenever she could get away.

He remembered one day in particular, a blazing summer day about two months after his visit from the Kellers, and on that day she had smiled absently as he handed her down from the saddle, and he could tell by the bleakness of her eyes that she was worried.

"Is anything the matter?" he asked.

"I . . . I'm not sure."

"Is it Otto and Jules?"

47

She had moved her shoulders, but she couldn't shrug the worry from her eyes. "Probably it isn't anything. It's just that they're so quiet, they're taking it so calmly when I expected an awful fight. It isn't like Otto and Jules to take a thing like this without hitting back."

She started shaking and wouldn't stop, even when he held her hard against him. "I'm behaving like a silly child," she said, not looking at him. Then she said a strange thing. "John, be powerful!" she said passionately. "Grow bigger than the Kellers, bigger than my father. I can't hold them back much longer."

After a long moment he said, "Don't you think you'd better start at the first and tell me about it?"

In order to explain it to him she had to go back a long way, all the way back to her childhood. Ever since she could remember, she said, Otto Keller had somehow managed to influence everything she did. It was strange, looking back on it, for he never said anything much, and he certainly never intimidated her, at least not directly.

Croy Hilderbrand was already a big man in Messina County when Otto and Jules were still wild cow-hunters in the Comanche country. At that time the Rocker-O was just a little barbed-wire outfit up on the northern reaches of Crazy Creek. People hardly knew the place was there at all until the Kellers started selling beef to the

Indian agents over in the New Mexico country; and by that time they were too big to scare out, the way the big ranchers would have done with ordinary nesters.

There was a time when people claimed that the Kellers weren't too particular about what kind of brand a cow wore, and rumor went about that both father and son were experts with wet blankets and running irons. But this was never proved, and it was never voiced in the presence of Otto and Jules, for they already had a reputation for toughness in a country where toughness was taken for granted.

It didn't occur to Myra for a long time, but she thought now that Otto had been in love with her from the very first, although he had never said so. When Myra was sixteen, Otto and Jules made a more or less formal call at the Double-O Star, and Otto had asked old Hilderbrand for his daughter's hand in marriage.

She thought it was very funny at the time. She had laughed when her father told her about it, because she couldn't imagine herself married to a man like Otto Keller, even if he was the last man in Messina County. Or in Texas, for that matter.

She was surprised and vaguely shocked when her father failed to see humor in the thing. He said Otto was a smart rancher and would eventually have a lot of money.

"I wish I could explain about Otto," she said

now, looking at him. "But there isn't much to tell, actually. It's hard to put into words."

One time, she remembered, she had ridden far out into the Hilderbrand south range to see a new colt which one of the riders had told her had been dropped by her favorite mare. It was a good half-day's ride from the Double-O Star, and it must have been more than thirty miles from the Keller headquarters. But when she got there, Otto was waiting. Unsmiling, stolid, sober. Heaven alone knew to what lengths he had gone in order to be at that particular place at that particular time. Then he spoke some insignificant words concerning the colt, the weather, the grass, and rode away.

John smiled thinly. In his mind he could see Otto doing it just that way.

Myra shook her head. He was always doing things like that, she said. He must have made his plans days in advance, spending hours on them, and for what? To look at her, to mumble a few incoherent words, and then ride away again. It was as though he was trying to break down her resistance merely by being in her presence as often as possible, hoping that sooner or later she would get used to him and accept him.

It was silly, she thought—but at the same time it was flattering too, having a man go to that much trouble, and knowing that someone loved her that much.

For a moment her eyes were blank, and then she closed them and gave an almost imperceptible shudder. "But I don't like him!" she said hoarsely. "I hate him. He's rough and coarse, and . . . My father must be insane, thinking I could ever marry a man like that."

"Did Otto keep bothering you?" Pasco asked. "Even after you told him to leave you alone?"

She hadn't actually told him, it turned out. That too was hard to explain, but she didn't want to make an enemy of him. It was almost as though she had known all along that someday she would depend on not being his enemy.

"Like now?" Pasco said.

She nodded. "I had no idea that it would be as simple as that, and maybe that's the thing that frightens me so. All I did was go to Otto and ask him to leave you alone. He looked at me in a funny kind of way, not saying anything, and then I told him I would never speak to him again if anything happened to you."

"Then what did he do?"

She shrugged. "He kind of smiled—as close as I ever saw him come to smiling—and he said whatever I wanted was fine with him."

"Does he know about us?"

"Yes."

"Did you tell him?"

"No. But he knows."

"Then it won't last." For some reason, he was

almost glad. He still didn't like the idea of having a girl protect him, fighting his fights for him. "He's just playing for time," Pasco said. "He doesn't want to turn you against him, but sooner or later he'll find another way."

Maybe she knew the things that were going around in his mind. "It's going to be all right, John. I know it will."

"I'd like to be that sure about it. You don't think Otto's going to just sit by, do you, while I graze out his south range and take away his girl?"

"I'm not his girl. I never was."

"But Otto doesn't know it."

She said abruptly, "John, do you love me?"

"You know I do."

"But you think it's hopeless, don't you? John, I told you that you'd be bigger than anybody in the county, and you will. You had the nerve to face up to the Rocker-O when all other ranchers were afraid to set foot on this part of the range. You wouldn't let them run you off, even when they beat you and burned you out. If you had been any other way, do you think I ever would have looked at you?"

Her smile vanished as she studied him. "It takes strong men to get ahead in this country," she went on. "No, I wouldn't even have looked at you if you had let Otto run you out of here. I'd have laughed at you." She took his arm, holding it tightly. "I know you have nothing now, but that doesn't mean anything. My father had nothing either, when he came to this country. And neither did Silas Hornsby or the Kellers. But they were strong men and they took what they wanted. That's the way you are—I knew it that day I saw you standing here in the midst of your burned-out camp, still ready to fight."

He said, a little sheepishly in spite of himself, "I guess I never looked at it that way. I never figured to be in competition with anybody, or fight anybody. I just did the thing that seemed to make some sense at the time. I don't know that I even want to be powerful."

"You can do it," she said positively, "and I'll tell you how. The important thing is to act fast, because I don't know how long I can hold Otto off. The first thing you have to do is hire some riders. You can get the kind I mean over in Indian Territory, or up in the Neutral Strip."

John's eyes widened. "You mean professional gunfighters, or ranch hands?"

"I mean you have to fight fire with fire. The Rocker-O has them on its payroll, and so do the other big outfits. You simply have to hire more and pay them better—it's the only kind of language the Kellers understand."

John Pasco shook his head. "Even if I was ready to do it," he said, "it would be impossible. I don't have the money to hire an ordinary ranch hand, for that matter."

"You can get it."

Pasco blinked. "How?"

"Do you know a man named Avery Slater?"

"The beef contractor for the Indian Agency?"

"Yes. He'll buy all the cattle you can round up."

Pasco looked at her, puzzled. "I couldn't round up more than a dozen head, and they're scattered all over the north of Texas."

"Listen to me." She sounded exasperated because he couldn't understand what she was getting at. "There's a bunch of cattle—four- or five-year-olds—over on the west range. I saw them only a few days ago. They were grazing in the draw where the Muleshoe bends to the north, and probably they're still there."

"I've seen them," Pasco said, "but they're not going to help me. They belong to the Rocker-O."

She looked at him without blinking. "I've seen this man Slater and I know what he's like. He'll buy the beef, if the price is right. The brand they wear doesn't make any difference."

Chapter Four

But that was long ago. Now, as John Pasco topped a small knoll, he knew the long ride from southwest Texas was ended. Shading his eyes with his hands, he stared out over the shimmering expanse of sun-scorched prairie. The town, a small huddle of frame buildings, was almost exactly as he remembered it.

Messina, like a great many towns in Texas, was built on a square. Around the square there was a box-shaped, disjointed string of buildings, there were raw planks discolored by the weather to varying shades of greys and browns. Shaky wooden awnings were attached to most of the storefronts, overhanging a battered plank walk. A few horses dozed at hitching racks or nosed gingerly at one of the four water troughs placed at each corner of the square.

In the center of the square stood a clumsy, two-story plank building, the Messina County Courthouse, its white paint blistered and peeling off in huge irregular patches. It was the place where John Pasco had been indicted on the charge of cattle rustling. Unconsciously, as he entered the town, his right hand went down to his cartridge belt, pulling his .45 around to the front where it would be easier to get at.

Trail-dirty, sweaty, he entered the town from

the south, his gaze flickering briefly at a small cluster of men loitering in front of the Stockman House Hotel. Halting their talk, they looked at him in vague curiosity, no recognition showing in their eyes. One of the men, a thin, taut reed of a man, was Karl Shoemire, the banker. He should recognize me, Pasco thought bleakly; he turned me down for loans plenty of times. Another of the group, a heavy-set man wearing black broadcloth, was Ed Bowman, owner of the Stockman House. He had been on the jury, but the man's face was blank. After a moment they all went back to talking.

There was a brass Napoleon cannon in front of the courthouse, a piece salvaged from some long-forgotten battle of the Civil War. Beside the cannon there was a small pyramid of iron solid-shot, held together with mortar. John Pasco reined up for a moment, staring at the cannon as though it held some special significance for him, but in his mind he was thinking of something else. He was thinking of the trial.

First an expert stock detective from the Cattlemen's Association had testified that a number of Rocker-O brands had been changed with a running iron to resemble Pasco's Muleshoe-P. By extending the sides of the Keller Rocker it was possible to produce a U similar to that part of Pasco's brand. To complete the brand change, all that was necessary was to burn a line down from the left side of the Keller O, making it a P. It was perfectly obvious, the prosecuting lawyer implied, that Pasco had selected the Muleshoe-P as his brand because it simplified the business of rustling.

Then Otto had produced hides bearing the botched brands, and the trial was over, as far as John Pasco was concerned. He was lucky to get off with three years, the Judge said. If it had happened in south Texas, they would have lynched him and the county would have been spared the expense of a court trial.

John Pasco sat through it, raging helplessly when he chanced to look at Otto Keller's impassive face. They're convinced he's telling the truth, he thought bitterly, looking at the jury. But he couldn't blame the jury. He had actually considered stealing those cattle once—maybe some of the guilt showed in his eyes and made it easier for them—but he hadn't done it!

Myra hadn't been at the trial. The last time he saw her was the day before the deputies from the sheriff's office came to arrest him.

"Well?" she had asked.

He didn't know what to answer. He had hardly slept for four nights. A dozen times he had almost decided to do as Myra wanted, steal the Rocker-O cows and sell them. She was right. In this country, a man had to take what he wanted, or he never got anywhere. But always, for some reason or other, he had put it off.

She said, "Have you seen Avery Slater?"

"No. Not yet."

Her eyes became anxious. "John, there isn't much time. I can't hold Otto off much longer; I can almost feel him getting away from me."

"There must be some other way. I guess I just wasn't cut out to be a rustler."

She stared at him. Suddenly her mouth curled faintly, almost in a sneer. "Don't be ridiculous," she said shortly. "You'll be doing nothing my own father didn't do. And most of the other ranchers in Texas, too, for that matter." Suddenly again, and unexpectedly, her voice became gentle. "John, we all have to fight for the things we want. Even steal, if we have to."

Then a great warmth swept over him and he held her in his arms for a long while. He loved her so much that the touch of her left him weak. He was tempted to ask her to marry him, right now, just the way he was, and to hell with the Kellers and Hilderbrands and all the rest of them.

He would have done it, but he knew it wouldn't do any good. She had already explained how she felt about that.

"Will you do it, John?"

"What if something goes wrong?"

She didn't answer. She had said it took a strong man to get what he wanted. Well, if something went wrong, it probably meant that he wasn't strong enough and she had been mistaken in thinking that he was.

So that was the way it ended. She didn't tell him that unless he did as she said, they were through, but that was what she meant. She rode away that day a little straighter than usual, her chin tilted a little more proudly.

She was leaving it up to him.

He thought it all out that night, lying on the slatted, straw-stuffed ticking of his bunk, and he decided that now was the time to break off with Myra. The best thing to do was forget her.

But forgetting her wasn't easy. He was young then, and he had never seen a girl like Myra before. He lay wide-eyed that night, with a lump inside him as hard and cold as a star.

As it turned out, the decision had been a quite unnecessary one, because Otto had taken things into his own hands by that time. He never knew exactly what it had been that made Otto change so suddenly from his position of passive resistance to attack. Maybe he knew Myra so well he could guess what was happening between them. Whatever it was, he didn't waste time once he made up his mind to strike. The rancher realized that another attack on Pasco, like the first one, would only make Myra more sympathetic and draw her closer to him. Instead, he had begun to create the evidence which would send Pasco to prison.

The sun was hardly up when two deputies came calling at his camp on the Muleshoe that morning.

"What do you want?" Pasco asked them.

"You're under arrest, Pasco." The deputy grinned, cradling a short-barreled carbine in his arm.

"What for?"

"You'll find out when we get you to the courthouse. . . ."

That was five years ago. Five centuries, five lifetimes. John Pasco came erect in the saddle, realizing that he had reined up in the middle of Messina's main street. Well, Otto, he thought, I'm back, finally. He nudged his horse, moving down the street toward the wagon yard.

After he had turned his horse into the wagon yard corral, he walked up the nearly deserted street, suddenly feeling the weight of trail dirt and grime, the accumulation of many days of travel. Feeling his stiff, inch-long beard, he realized why no one had recognized him. The dirt, the beard, the narrow-brimmed hat—he grinned thinly at his reflection in a window. No wonder people had stopped their conversations to look at him.

He stopped once before the swinging doors of a saloon, listened for a moment to the murmur of voices inside, then walked on. His throat was dry and raw with prairie grit and he could have used a drink, but he needed a bath worse.

There used to be a barber shop and bath house at the northwest corner of the square, he remembered. He headed in that direction, quartering across the dirt street as a buckboard rattled to a stop by the hitching rack.

Stepping up to the plank walk again, he stood uncertainly, looking for the barber shop. Maybe they moved it, he thought. Then he saw the scaling red-and-white striped pole. He started toward it when a voice called out, startlingly clear in the quiet of the afternoon.

"John! John Pasco!"

He didn't recognize her at first. She stood in the doorway of a store, a strange half-smile touching the corners of her mouth. For a moment Pasco searched the back of his mind, trying to place her. She wasn't pretty exactly, but there was a cleanness and erectness about her that he liked. Her hair was light, almost a wheat color, with life to it, and her eyes were clear and direct and honest.

Then Pasco saw the velvet pin cushion strapped to her left arm. He noticed the draped figure in the small store window and the swinging sign over the door which said, in peeling letters: Ladies' Wear Emporium.

Pasco smiled faintly, a bit self-consciously. "Why, hello, Peg."

"John, it's really you. I wasn't sure at first."

"Huntsville changes men some," he said bluntly,

and was vaguely surprised when she didn't seem flustered or uncomfortable at his mention of the prison.

She said evenly, "I was making some coffee in the back. Will you have a cup with me?"

"I was headed for the barber shop," he said. "I'll drop in later, though, if the offer still holds."

"It does."

They stood there for an awkward moment—awkward for John Pasco, at least. In the past, if he had thought of Peg Manning at all it had been as a rowdy, rather loud-mouthed tomboy. She wasn't a tomboy now—not by a long way.

"Well—"

"Later, then," she said.

"All right. . . ."

Settling into the barber chair, Pasco said, "I want to take a bath, too, if you can get somebody to rustle up some hot water."

The barber went to the front door and called to someone down the street, and pretty soon a boy of eleven or twelve came in, staggering under the weight of two buckets of water. The boy went back to the bathroom and began stoking the wood-burning stove.

Not until the beard was gone and the hair cut—short on top and clipped straight up the temples—did the barber stand back and say, "Haven't I seen you somewhere before, mister?"

"I guess so. I used to live here."

"Then you're John Pasco," he said, looking startled.

"That's right," Pasco said flatly. "Now if the water's ready, I'll get on with the bath."

The bathroom was the second room of the barber shop. Pasco stood just inside the door watching the boy pour the two steaming buckets of water into a round wooden tub. After he had pulled up a wooden dressing bench, laid out a towel, topped it with a cake of yellow soap, Pasco peeled some bills off the small roll he had.

"Do you think you can get me some new clothes?"

The boy looked up. "Sure." It was part of his job. Cowhands, after spending a long time on the trail or on the range, didn't often bother to have their old clothes washed when they hit town. They bought new ones if they were lucky enough to get to the bath house before the fancy women or a gambling house took their pay.

Pasco spent almost a full hour in the tub, feeling himself relax slowly. As he dried himself and began pulling on the new suit of underwear he thought, well, it's probably all over town by now, that John Pasco has come back with a gun on his hip. Otto will probably get the word before nightfall. News traveled like that in a country where there was little enough to talk about.

But at that moment he was unconcerned with Otto. He tucked his fresh blue hickory shirt inside the cheap cotton pants; then he pulled on his boots, after first wiping them with the discarded towel. Finally he picked up his gunbelt, swung it around his waist and buckled it.

When he came out of the bathroom, he broke up a small group of men who had suddenly found the barber shop an interesting place to be. They were talking and motioning in various stages of excitement—but all talk stopped suddenly the moment John entered the room.

"How much do I owe you?" he said to the barber.

"Two dollars, including the bath," the man said, looking uncomfortable.

Pasco paid him, walked toward the door, feeling a dozen curious eyes on his back. Impulsively, he stopped before stepping out to the walk and turned to face them.

"Why don't you go over to the boneyard with the other vultures?" he said flatly. "There's nobody dead here, yet." Their eyes popped, but no one said a word.

Pasco stepped outside. It's just as well I came with a gun, he thought. They wouldn't have had it any other way!

He had completely forgotten Peg Manning and his promise to take coffee with her. He started across the street toward an eating house, when she called to him again, startling him for the second time that day.

"John Pasco, I do believe you're trying to dodge me."

He turned, grinning. "I guess I haven't got much of a memory." He walked heavily back to the store front where she was standing. "I'm glad you stopped me, though. I was about to poison myself with some of that stuff they pass out as coffee in eating houses."

She smiled. She wouldn't be called a pretty girl—handsome was more like it. Peg was rather a large girl, only an inch or so shorter than Pasco himself. Her hair was a dark blonde. He found himself liking her, thinking that she was the kind of girl that a man could laugh with, but would never want to marry, probably. She looked strong enough to whip most men.

Awkwardly, he followed Peg through the dress shop, aware that he was in a place meant for women, a place where most men refused to tread. Dress forms stood partially draped, bristling with pins. The floor around the cutting bench at the back of the store was littered with remnants of varicolored materials and pieces of tissue paper dress patterns. Shelves in the back were loaded with bolts of new cloth, and the clean, dry smell peculiar to new drygoods was mingled vaguely with the heavier odor of coffee.

"Your mother," Pasco said, mainly to break the silence, "I hope she's well."

Peg looked back, a faint look of surprise in her

eyes. "She died," she said. "Three years ago."

"Oh."

At the back of the store there was a curtained partition, and on the other side of the curtain there was a sitting room, and beyond that a kitchen. Pasco had been in the kitchen before, a few times, but that was long ago. He dimly remembered Mrs. Manning—a stout, laughing woman—handing out fresh rolls to Peg and other kids at the back door.

"Sit down," Peg said.

He sat down at a round oak table. Peg set out canned milk, sugar and thick china cups, then she poured from a blue enameled coffee pot and sat across from him.

She glanced down at her coffee. "You've changed, John," she said.

"How?"

"I don't know. Your eyes are narrower, your mouth thinner. You look as if you haven't laughed for a long time."

"I'm what they call a hardcase," he said, attempting a grin that didn't quite come off.

"I guessed that much by the way you wear your gun. Did you come back to Messina to kill Otto Keller?"

He laughed then, without humor. "You come right out with what's on your mind, don't you?"

"Did you?"

"Well, if he asks for trouble, I'll be ready."

"And you'll see that he asks for it, won't you?"

Pasco frowned. "What is this, an inquisition? I'm in town less than an hour and you're about the fifth person to suggest that I've come gunning for Otto."

Peg Manning sighed. "They've been expecting you, more or less, for two years. They thought if you were coming back, it would be right after they let you out of prison."

"What are you trying to tell me, Peg?"

"Just that Otto's the biggest man in this part of Texas these days, bigger than Hilderbrand, even, or Silas Hornsby. Old Jules died last winter; since then Otto has been spreading the Rocker-O all over the Panhandle. Both Otto and Hilderbrand are warring with Silas Hornsby now, trying to force his Crazy Creek brand off the range—and they'll do it, too, before long."

Pasco said slowly, "I don't see what this has to do with me."

"You didn't come back just on Otto's account. Other people may be blind, but I'm not, John. And Otto isn't either."

"What is that supposed to mean?"

"Otto knew about you and Myra Hilderbrand." John Pasco came out of his chair at that, and Peg grinned. "I was guessing, of course, but you were in love with Myra, weren't you? And she was probably in love with you, or thought she was. I got to thinking about it all after the trial, and

67

that was the only way it would work out. Everybody knows Otto was always crazy about Myra. Everybody knows too that Otto wouldn't have let you stay on the Muleshoe as long as you did unless he had a good reason. The reason was Myra."

John sat back, studying her. "Peg," he said finally, "you sure do take some wild guesses."

"But they're pretty good ones, aren't they?"

"All right," he said, "they're pretty good guesses, but I still don't see what it has to do with things now."

"Are you still in love with Myra?"

He rubbed his face with his hand, still wondering what he was doing here, talking this way to a girl he remembered only fuzzily from his childhood. It was a good feeling, though, being able to talk about it like this, knowing instinctively that it would never go farther than the kitchen. Maybe, he thought, I should have talked about it long ago.

"I don't know how I feel about her," he said at last. "Peg, that's the truth."

She shook her head slowly.

"All right," he said wearily. "I guess I do love her. But that doesn't have anything to do with me and Otto."

"That's where you're wrong," Peg Manning said. "Her name is Keller now. She married Otto last spring."

Chapter Five

It was the quiet time of day for the Stockman House. A town idler slouched at the bar watching Pasco curiously in the backbar mirror. The bartender was polishing glasses. Pasco had a table in the corner of the room, and the bottle in front of him was less than half full. It had been full a little more than an hour ago when he had first sat down.

So she finally married Otto, he thought, staring at his glass. Well, she picked the biggest man in the Panhandle, anyway. That was bound to happen, I guess.

He poured himself another drink. His stomach growled for food, but food could never give him the feeling of warmth and security that came from the bottle. He stuck to whiskey.

One thing whiskey did for a man—it eliminated the many small unimportant things in his mind and brought to a head the really important things. Pasco thought, there was a time once when I had a place to go after the day's work was done. It wasn't much, but it was mine. It's Otto's now.

It was as simple as that. When he got to thinking about it, he always got around to Otto. For a long while he sat without moving, letting the anger have its way inside him.

With an effort, he shook off some of his heaviness and anger. He pushed the bottle away, put both hands on the tabletop and started to lift himself out of the chair.

"Your name Pasco?" a man said. He was a big, raw-boned, loose-lipped man who had just come into the bar. His face was sweaty and his eyes were hard and there was a silver-plated town marshal's star pinned to the flap of his shirt pocket. There was a Colt .45 in his hand.

"That's my name," Pasco said after a moment. "What's the gun for?"

"Just stand up and turn around."

"Like hell!" But it was the whiskey talking. No man in his right mind would argue with the muzzle of a .45. Before he could move, before he could say another word, the gunbarrel flashed. The marshal grunted as he whipped the heavy handful of steel into Pasco's face.

Pasco reeled back, numbed for a moment by the blow. Almost instantly the bartender had come around the bar with a sawed-off shotgun.

"Now no more of that," the marshal said mildly. "You're in enough trouble as it is."

Dumbly, Pasco realized that it would be suicide to make a move toward his gun. The muzzle of the bartender's sawed-off was pressed against his back. Quickly, with expert hands, the marshal went over him, lifting his revolver from the holster. "Now," the marshal said, satisfied, "we'll go."

Pasco held his anger in. There would be time

enough for that later. "If it's not too much trouble," he said dryly, "I'd like to know what this is all about."

"That's simple enough." The marshal smiled. "You're disturbing the peace."

"What did I do to disturb the peace?"

"You can think that over in jail." The marshal waved his gun. "Let's go, nice and quiet."

There were only a few idlers on the plank walk as they cut across the dusty street toward the courthouse. They stared curiously at the cut on Pasco's face, but offered no comment—at least not until the marshal had ushered Pasco through the front door of the courthouse. His rage still locked tight inside him, Pasco allowed himself to be nudged through the semidarkness of a long hallway to the back of the building, where the marshal's office and the jail cells were.

He murmured once, "Your justice doesn't change much here in Messina, does it?"

The marshal only grunted. With one hand he lighted a coal oil lamp and placed it on top of a rolltop desk. He carefully kept his .45 leveled at Pasco as he did it.

"How long do you aim to keep me locked up for doing nothing?" Pasco asked flatly.

The marshal took a ring of heavy keys and motioned him toward the back of the office, where three empty cells were waiting. "That depends," he said mildly. He waved Pasco into an end cell, clanged the barred door into place and locked it. For a moment he smiled blankly, without malice. "Anyway," he said, "our jail isn't so bad. Some of our customers claim the Stockman House beds are softer, but all in all we don't get many complaints."

Pasco said nothing. There was no arguing with iron bars and drawn revolvers. He wondered for a moment if Otto's power now reached into the marshal's office, and then decided that the marshal was his own man. He was tough, Pasco decided. He could be mean if he felt like it, but he was hardly the kind of man to take orders from Otto Keller, or from anybody else.

Pasco sat on the narrow bunk at the back of the cell, licking a cigarette into shape as the marshal tramped heavily out of the office. Holding a match to his smoke, he thought: maybe it happened for the best, after all. At least the marshal got me away from the bottle. Otto would have loved it, coming up on me after I was half drunk. If he had, there would have been a fresh grave in boothill by this time tomorrow—and it wouldn't have been Otto's.

The thought hardened inside him. Yes, maybe the marshal had done him a bigger favor than he knew.

After a while the marshal came back with a cloth-covered platter and a small syrup bucket half full of coffee.

"You've got a visitor," he said.

Pasco felt himself stiffen. It wouldn't be Otto, he thought. He wouldn't come here. And it wouldn't be—Myra. The marshal unlocked the cell door and handed the platter and coffee inside. "It's Hornsby," he said.

"Who?"

"Silas Hornsby, the owner of the Crazy Creek brand." The marshal locked the door again. "I saw him over at the Stockman House and he wanted to know if he could talk to you. I told him it would be up to you."

For a moment Pasco stared thoughtfully at the hot platter in his hands—steak and fried potatoes and biscuits. He had never had anything to do with the Crazy Creek owner. He knew Hornsby to speak to, but that was all. It didn't make much sense that a big rancher like that would have anything to say to him.

"Well?" the marshal said.

"All right. I've got plenty of time, it looks like. If Hornsby wants to talk to me, I don't mind."

The marshal grinned without humor, then he went to the front of the office and called into the hallway. "All right, Hornsby."

Chapter Six

The rancher, a squat, soft-bellied man with pale eyes and thinning grey hair came in, nodding briefly to the marshal. "If you don't mind, Bunt," he said, "this is personal."

Pasco said, "I've got no personal life to speak of. I don't mind if the marshal listens in." He had never particularly liked Hornsby, principally because of the soft, jellish look of the man. But somewhere, Pasco knew, inside those flabby folds of flesh, there was a core of ruthlessness. Without it, he would never have become the power he was in Messina County. Placing his platter on the bunk and the bucket of coffee on the floor at his feet, Pasco said, "What's on your mind, Hornsby?"

"Well." He glanced over his shoulder at the marshal, who was seating himself at the rolltop desk. "Pasco, I'm here to offer you a job."

Pasco blinked. "What kind of a job?"

"I'm hiring at the Crazy Creek, when I can find the right kind of man." Pasco noticed that small beads of sweat were forming on the rancher's forehead.

Pasco cut into his steak and said, "Isn't this the slack time of year to be hiring new riders?"

Hornsby laughed shortly. "The ranches around

here are hiring, all right. Not only my place, but the Rocker-O and the Double-O Star too."

Pasco didn't get it, but apparently the marshal did. He turned slowly in his chair until he was facing the cell, his face blank. "Hornsby," he said, "I didn't try to stop you from coming here because I knew that sooner or later you'd get your proposition across anyway. If he wants to sign on with you, I guess I can't stop that either. But sooner or later somebody's going to step across the line, and when that happens—"

He left the rest unsaid. Lifting himself out of the chair, he walked out of the office without looking at either of them.

Pasco said, "What was that for?"

Hornsby wiped his forehead with a blue bandanna, and Pasco noticed that his eyes were slitted and quick, like the eyes of a well-fed cat. "Bunt Wallace has got pretty high and mighty," the rancher said, almost to himself.

"Is that the marshal's name?"

Hornsby nodded. "Some of the townspeople weren't satisfied with the way the county sheriff was doing things, so they hired Wallace on as a special marshal. A mistake, if you ask me. He keeps sticking his nose into things that are none of his business."

Pasco touched his bruised face where Wallace had pistol-whipped him. He was tough, all right but maybe a tough marshal was what Messina needed. After a moment he said, "What did he mean that sooner or later somebody was going to step across the line?"

"Wallace doesn't have any authority outside Messina's city limits." The rancher's voice trailed off. He hadn't come here to talk about Bunt Wallace. "About that job I mentioned. It's yours, if you want it."

"Thanks just the same," Pasco said. "I'm not looking for a job right now."

Hornsby paused, then said, "But you're looking for Otto Keller, aren't you?"

"Everybody seems to think so. Even if I am, what's this job got to do with it?"

Hornsby smiled for the first time. "For one thing, you'll never get Otto in Messina. The minute Bunt heard that Otto was coming to town, you'd land in jail until he left, just the way you did today. I've got no love for special marshals, but you can bet there won't be any fights in Messina as long as Bunt's on the job."

Then the rancher lost his smile, and his beefy face took on a sober look. "Of course," he said, "maybe I'm wrong and you've got nothing against Otto. But if you have, Messina's no place to settle with him. And outside Messina is no place, either, if you're by yourself. Maybe you haven't heard, but the Rocker-O is a hardcase crew now, with every rider with the outfit drawing fighting pay. Hilderbrand's Double-O

Star is almost as bad. How long do you think you'd last going up against crews like them?"

Pasco was beginning to get it now. He remembered the range war that Peg Manning had mentioned.

Pasco studied Hornsby's shifting eyes. His first impulse was to reach through the bars and take the rancher by his fat throat and shake him like a terrier shaking a rat. He didn't like hired gunmen, and he didn't intend to be one. Still—

Gradually his anger dissolved and became lost in the greater anger he held for Otto. He reasoned, I can't blame Hornsby for taking me for a hardcase; everybody else has. He sat on the bunk for a long while, saying nothing, turning the thing over in his mind. What difference did it make where it happened, how it happened. He laughed shortly. You don't have to worry about your reputation, Pasco. That was taken care of long ago. By Otto.

Hornsby was waiting patiently. At last Pasco said, "I can't be sure now. I'll have to think it over."

"That's all right. You'll be safe enough as long as Bunt keeps you locked up."

"What does that mean?"

"Well . . ." The rancher shrugged. "I don't know how true it is, but the story has it that Otto and some of his boys are ready for you. They're

77

just waiting for you to set foot outside Messina city limits."

Pasco felt his mouth draw thin. "I'll take care of myself."

Shrugging again, the rancher turned to go. "Just the same, I'll keep some of my riders in town until you make up your mind. Pasco, I've got a feeling that between the two of us we can beat Hilderbrand and Keller and anybody else they want to bring into it—because we both hate them. Hired guns are all right, but nothing takes the place of hate when it's tooth and nail. Well, think it over. You'll get top pay, of course, if you decide to throw in with us."

The rancher walked out and Pasco listened to the heavy clack of his bootheels in the empty courthouse. At last, pushing the platter and coffee to one side, he lay across the bunk, staring up at the high plank ceiling of the cell. His whole plan had suddenly lost its neatness and simplicity. The Messina range war, if there was one, was none of his business. But it seemed that he would be forced to make it his business if he meant to get at Otto. One man couldn't fight an army.

He had no love for Hornsby, but he held no hate for him, as he did Keller. And Myra . . . He couldn't be sure what she meant to him now. But he could feel the emptiness when he thought of her. Until now he had not allowed himself to think of her as Otto's wife. But the picture was there, on the outer edges of his mind, waiting for the opening that had to come. He could glimpse it now—Otto's rough hands on the paleness of her shoulders, demanding his rights as a husband. Otto's thick, bruising mouth against Myra's . . . Well, Pasco thought with bitterness, a strong man was what you wanted, Myra.

He felt relief when the marshal came back into the office and he could turn his mind to something else.

Bunt Wallace took his tilt-back chair and sat facing his desk for several moments without speaking. Finally he turned, and his eyes held a grimness now that Pasco hadn't noticed before. He said, "Well, did you decide to hire out to Hornsby?"

"I haven't decided," Pasco said. "There'll be time for that when I get out of jail."

The marshal waited a long moment before speaking again. Then he took the cell keys from a desk drawer and said, "You're free to go any time you feel like it. It looks like Otto Keller won't be coming into Messina for a while. He and Hilderbrand just started themselves a war with Hornsby's outfit, looks like." He sounded tired and disinterested. "Keller's Rocker-O crew dammed up Crazy Creek above the Hornsby grazing range, so the story goes."

Pasco sat up on his bunk. "Was there a fight?"

"Two Crazy Creek riders just brought one of

their boys in with a .30-30 bullet in his lung. Doc Fuller's working on him now at the hotel, but it's my guess we'll be having a funeral tomorrow." He walked over to the cell, unlocked the door and swung it open, grinning cynically.

"I'm free?" Pasco asked, still not believing it could happen so fast.

"You're free. But Lord help you, Pasco, if you try to bring your private war to Messina."

Pasco walked out of the cell and the marshal handed him his .45 and cartridge belt. As Pasco buckled on his gun the marshal went over to his desk and stood there looking at the plank wall. After a moment, not turning, he said, "You want a piece of advice, Pasco?"

Pasco said nothing for a moment, and the marshal said, "I'll give it to you anyway. Get out of Messina. Not just the town, the county, and this part of Texas. I know about your record, but I'm not in the habit of judging a man by what I hear." He stopped suddenly, turning, his face hot in sudden anger. "Oh, hell, get out of here!"

It was dark as he walked from the courthouse, and although there were several men gathered in front of the Stockman House, the night seemed heavy and quiet. Pasco walked across the brittle, parched grass of the square, toward a group of men gathered on the hotel porch. An old man, grey and stooped, stood in the hotel doorway mopping his face with a soiled bandanna. The sleeves of his black alpaca coat were pushed up and his cuffs turned back, revealing blood-stained hands. Pasco recognized the old man as Doc Fuller.

"How's the patient, Doc?" Someone called out from the darkness.

"Dead," the doctor said flatly, and began carefully to roll down his sleeves.

The crowd began to break up, still quiet, solemn. Few of their faces showed surprise, or any other emotion, for that matter. The war had been threatening for years, and now that it had finally arrived it was almost an anticlimax.

Pasco stood by himself at the edge of the dispersing crowd, not wanting to go back into the Stockman House, and not knowing where else to go. At last he turned and began walking away from the hotel, and not for several moments did he realize that he was heading for the corral where he had left his horse.

He paused for a moment, thoughtfully, and then began retracing his steps toward the Stockman House. When he reached the front porch of the hotel, he was surprised to see Peg Manning coming out of the building. She looked at him blankly, her hair disarrayed, the sleeves of her cotton dress pushed up to her elbows. Under her arm she held a newspaper-wrapped bundle that Pasco took to be an apron.

"Oh," she said, sounding surprised. Then she smiled faintly, but the smile didn't reach her eyes. "I've been helping the doctor," she said. "There didn't seem to be anyone else." She made an unconscious gesture of straightening her hair. "I guess I'm not much of a nurse," she went on, strangely without emotion, and then her voice trailed off.

Pasco wanted to say something to reassure her. It couldn't have been very pleasant for her, watching a man die and not being able to do anything about it. But if there was any hysteria inside her, she kept it from showing. He looked at her, and then at the swinging doors of the saloon. "I don't suppose Hornsby is in there, is he?"

She looked at him abstractedly, her mind still on something else. "No," she said. "He and his riders headed back to the Crazy Creek head-quarters as soon as—"

As soon as the Crazy Creek rider died—but she didn't say it. Pasco stood uneasily for a moment. Well, there's no particular hurry, he thought. The war would wait for him. Otto Keller would wait. He said, with such gentleness as he could muster, "I'll see you home, Peg."

He took the bundle from her, and without speaking, they started slowly up the plank walk, toward Peg's dress shop. Finally Pasco said, wanting to change the subject, "I had a run-in with the town marshal today. But I guess you heard about that."

She nodded. "Bunt Wallace is all right. We wouldn't have the range war now, if he were the sheriff."

"Where did he come from? Does anyone know anything about him?"

"Not much," Peg said, shaking her head. "He came from Kansas, so the story goes. But nobody knows for sure. Two years ago he tried his hand at barbed-wire ranching down south, but he couldn't make a go of it. Nobody can down there. Later he got on here as special marshal."

They walked on in silence for a few moments, until they reached the dress shop.

"I have some more coffee," Peg said half-heartedly, but Pasco shook his head.

"Maybe some other time."

He watched her open the shop door and light a lamp inside. As the flame from the wick flared up he was surprised to see how tired she looked. He felt a crazy impulse to smooth her hair—and then he smiled to himself. Not unless you want to get your face slapped, Pasco. Instead, he touched the brim of his hat.

"Good night, Peg."

She said nothing for a moment. Then turned holding the lamp in her hand. "I hear you're joining with Crazy Creek," she said with her usual bluntness.

Surprised, Pasco laughed. "It looks like you got the story before I did."

Her face showed no expression. "Are you?" she asked.

What could you say to a woman like that? "I—I don't know," he said finally. There was nothing more to say, and finally he touched his hat again and turned and walked back toward the Stockman House.

He kept going this time, walking past the hotel and into the darkness beyond the square, along the rutted stage road that led past the livery barn. Women! he thought, half in anger, half in wonder. As he walked, he glanced up at the scattering of stars. Nine o'clock, he thought. No later than that. Within luck at all, he could reach the Crazy Creek headquarters before midnight, about the same time he figured Hornsby and his riders would get there.

Up ahead he could see the livery corral looming out of the darkness. Then, abruptly, a small sound stopped him. A very small sound, lost somewhere in the bigness of the night—but the metallic click of a rifle hammer being drawn back slowly was unmistakable.

Acting on instinct, Pasco flung himself down onto the clay road, and almost instantly a rifle spat fire from the direction of the livery corral. The explosion split the night like a ripe melon. Pasco rolled over, grabbing at his .45. The rifle crashed again, but in a different place this time, and Pasco guessed that the gunman was retreating farther back into the darkness.

Somehow the revolver was now in Pasco's hand. He felt it buck once, twice, three times, the explosions shattering the night. He knew that nothing but luck and darkness saved him, but luck and darkness worked both ways. He couldn't see the gunman. He could only hear the nervous scampering of iron-shod hoofs as he shoved himself up from the ground and began running toward the corral.

He was too late. Even now he could hear the creak of saddle leather as the gunman swung aboard, and only then did he see the shapeless figure of rider and horse disappear behind the livery barn. Knowing it was useless, Pasco fired once more as a man, cursing furiously, appeared in the doorway of the barn.

"What the hell!" he bellowed.

Pasco was working frantically at the rope latch on the corral, and the stableman charged down on him.

"Hold on there, damn you!" the stableman shouted. Pasco could see now that he was a bearded old-timer, his suspenders hanging, his long underwear buttoned tightly about his scrawny throat. And finally Pasco saw the shot-gun that the old stableman was waving wildly in front of him.

"I've got to get my horse," Pasco shouted.

"Forget the horse!" The old man spat. "An' don't make a move, unless you want to feel the wind blowing through your middle."

Pasco stood in helpless rage, listening to the rapid beat of hoofs diminishing in the darkness. "I tell you that man tried to kill me. I've got a right to go after him!"

The old man grunted. He had the situation under control now, and he knew it. "I reckon I'm the one to decide who goes after who. An' I ain't deciding nothing till the marshal gets here."

Already they could hear the confused clatter of bootheels on the clay road, coming from the direction of the square. But the sound of the rifleman's horse had already vanished to the south. For a moment Pasco felt the helplessness of rage. It gnawed at him as he stood for one wild moment, his gun in his hand. But he couldn't kill the old man, and he didn't dare make a move as long as the stableman had the ugly twin muzzles of the shotgun pointed at his middle.

Pasco had expected Bunt Wallace to be the first person to reach the scene of the shooting, but most of the men of the town had gathered before the marshal finally arrived. When he saw that it was Pasco, he didn't seem surprised. "You don't stay out of trouble very long, do you?" he said dryly. "Was that you doing the shooting?"

"Part of it. But I didn't start it until somebody

tried to bushwhack me from over there by the corral."

The marshal looked at him with his hard eyes and Pasco could see that he didn't believe him. Shootings didn't happen in a place where Bunt Wallace was marshal. For a moment, though, he said nothing. Then finally he turned to the crowd of idlers who were crowding around. "Whatever it was," he said, "it's all over now. I'll take care of it."

There were a few disgruntled murmurings and nervous scraping of boots, but the crowd began to break up. If there had been any doubt in Pasco's mind as to who was boss in Messina, there was none now. Wallace ruled the town with an iron hand.

Without looking at the stableman, the marshal said, "Get me a lantern." Then, to Pasco, "If there was any bushwhacking, which I doubt, there'll be evidence a-plenty. And if there wasn't—"

He left the rest unsaid. With a practiced motion, as easy as lighting a cigarette, the marshal flicked Pasco's .45 out of the holster and shoved it into his own waistband. "It seems like this is getting to be a habit," he said tonelessly, moving his head slightly, in a command for Pasco to follow him.

The old man came back from the barn, carrying a lighted lantern, and this time Pasco was glad to see that he had left his shotgun behind. "Over there by the corral," the marshal said. "That's where he says the shooting came from."

The stableman spat disgustedly. "Don't know why you go to all this trouble. Wasn't no rifle shooting or I would have heard it. I heard the shooting and when I came out of the livery barn there wasn't nobody there but just this jasper. Must be plumb crazy, if you ask me, shooting off his gun in the dead of the night."

Wallace grinned thinly. "We'll see."

The crowd was straggling back toward the square as the marshal and Pasco and the old stableman moved deeper into the darkness, toward a circular pole corral.

"This the place?" Wallace asked.

"Over to the right, I think."

They walked on a few more steps, searching the crowd carefully in the circle of orange light cast by the lantern. "Wait a minute," Pasco said. The packed clay was torn by iron-shod hoofs. Pasco straightened and looked back to the road where he had been when the shooting took place.

He glanced at the marshal. "This is the place, all right."

The old stableman said, "Can't tell nothing about them shoe marks. Horses go back and forth across here all day."

The marshal said nothing, but continued swinging the lantern from side to side in long arcs as he scanned the area. Suddenly he grunted, bent over and picked something off the ground.

Pasco came forward. "What is it?"

The marshal handed him a brass cartridge case, and Pasco smiled faintly. Maybe his luck was changing for the better. "Thirty-thirty," he said. "Winchester, probably, and it's still warm. Does that convince you, Marshal?"

"Maybe." It was said reluctantly, and Pasco guessed the marshal's confidence in himself as a peace officer had been shaken. At last he handed the lantern back to the old stableman. "That's all for now," he said, and the old man headed back toward the barn.

Wallace took a minute to roll a cigarette. Then, as he held a flaring match to its tip, he said, "You headed anywhere in particular, Pasco, when the shooting started?"

"To the livery corral to pick up my horse."

"You were going up toward Crazy Creek?"

"Is there anything wrong with that?"

The marshal shrugged. That part had been straightened out as far as he was concerned. "You got any ideas about who the bushwhacker was?"

"I guess that's clear enough. You find Otto Keller and you'll find the owner of the .30-30 that just cut down on me."

Again the marshal shrugged. "Maybe. But I think you're wrong about Otto. He's got all the fighting he wants right now trying to hold that dam he put across Hornsby's branch of Crazy Creek."

"He's got men hired to do his fighting for him. He could have ridden into Messina tonight. You were expecting him to do just that; it was the reason you had me jailed."

The tip of the marshal's cigarette glowed in the darkness. "That was before I heard about the range war. Anyway, it doesn't sound much like Otto, waiting in the dark to shoot a man in the back."

Pasco said nothing. He felt the marshal watching him calmly, coldly, and finally he handed Pasco his .45. "I reckon you'd better get your horse, at that," he said flatly. "The sooner you get out of Messina, the better." He turned on his heel and marched off toward the square.

Methodically, Pasco punched the empty shell cases out of his .45 and replaced them with fresh rounds from his cartridge belt. Slipping the revolver back in his holster, he turned and started toward the livery barn to pick up his gear.

Chapter Seven

The small stream that gave the Crazy Creek brand its name started far above the Hornsby grazing range, furnishing both Keller's Rocker-O and Hornsby's herds with all-important water. Below the Hornsby range Crazy Creek crossed with the Muleshoe, but that was on Hilderbrand property—according to Hilderbrand's liberal interpretation of free range.

This was familiar land to Pasco, as he rode steadily north from Messina, across the Muleshoe, finally across the twisting, erratic stream of Crazy Creek, which was generally adjudged to belong to Hornsby. Toward midnight a pale moon made its appearance and stared coldly down upon the land, and Pasco got his first glimpse of the Hornsby headquarters.

Remembering the attempted ambush, Pasco had traveled carefully from Messina, skirting the wagon road most of the way, holding closely to the low ridges, such as they were in that flat country. But now he could relax. The Hornsby headquarters buildings lay sprawled in the bottom of a shallow depression set away slightly from the creek bed. Pasco sat quietly for several moments, watching the hurried activity which was so unusual at that time of night on a working ranch.

He could see the rosy glow of cook house fires, and flickering lights of lamps and lanterns were showing in windows of most of the buildings.

Pasco touched his own mount and moved in closer to the activity. But before he reached the pole fence fronting the headquarters building, a voice called out from the darkness, "Hold on there, mister!"

Pasco reined up, seeing the rider coming toward him, holding a short carbine at the ready across his saddlehorn.

The rider stopped at a careful distance and drawled flatly, "Haven't you heard that this is a bad time for night riding?"

Pasco straightened in the saddle, but he couldn't tell much about the man until he came closer. "My name is Pasco. Hornsby offered me a job in town today."

"Ain't this a funny time to start looking for work?"

"It's a funny hour to have a ranch going full blast, for that matter. Call Hornsby. He'll vouch for me."

The rider laughed softly, without much humor. But he still wasn't sure. With the Rocker-O warring with them only a few miles up the creek, Hornsby's men had become suspicious of everything that moved. Finally he said, "Mister, I just hope you're what you claim to be." Then he called out, "Somebody send Silas over here!"

After a moment three riders cut away from the corrals and headed toward them. One of the men called, "That you Carl?"

The man holding Pasco called back, "You hire on anybody in town today?"

Silas Hornsby reined up with two men, squinting his eyes in the darkness. At last he recognized Pasco and grunted with satisfaction. "I figured maybe you'd be coming around."

Pasco nodded. "I decided to take that job you offered, if it's still open."

Hornsby grunted. "It's open, all right. All hell's broke loose up north. We're getting ready to dynamite Otto's dam."

"Tonight?"

"As soon as I can get the men up there. The creek's already dry. By this time tomorrow my cattle will be bawling for water. I'll sign you on the payroll in the morning, if that's all right."

Pasco nodded.

Hornsby turned to the man called Carl. "He's all right. Take him over to the cook shack and give him anything he needs. In about thirty minutes he'll pull out with the rest of us." Hornsby wheeled his horse and his two men flanked him immediately, like trained dragoons. Then, as an afterthought, the rancher said, "Maybe you'll get your chance at Otto tonight, Pasco. The sooner the better, as far as I'm concerned."

Carl slipped his carbine back toward the saddle

boot, grinning thinly as Hornsby and his two riders headed back toward headquarters. He was a long, gaunt-faced man with an enormous hooked nose as sharp as a scalping knife. Even in the darkness, his deep-set eyes seemed bright and faintly amused as he leaned across his horse's neck and extended a work-roughened hand to Pasco.

"I don't know why anybody would want to join up in this private war," he drawled, "but I'll say this much—you're welcome. I'm Carl Levi, Hornsby's foreman."

Pasco took the man's big hand. "I'm John Pasco. I hear Hornsby's pay is good. That's enough reason for a man to join on."

"Fighting pay's all right, but it's not enough in a war like this one. Not if there's something else you can do." But he grinned as he said it, taking the sting of accusation out of his words. "Do you want to ride up to the cook shack? I'll get you a grub sack and some extra ammunition, if you need it."

They nudged their horses up a gentle slope, riding through an opened rail gate in front of the Hornsby ranch house. The cook shack was a lean-to affair at the back of the main ranch building. Pasco and Levi dismounted, falling into a short line of riders waiting for the cook to get their grub sacks ready.

A voice, probably the wrangler's, called out

from somewhere. "Extra ammunition in front of the headquarters building. Come and get it!"

The riders gulped scalding coffee from tin cups, picked up their grub sacks containing bacon and cornbread, and trotted toward the front of the headquarters building. Pasco and Levi picked up their own sacks, and Levi said, "I'll get the wrangler to rustle up a fresh mount. You may need it before the night's over."

"Could I get some corn for my own horse?"

"Sure. We've got more corn than water right now."

Pasco glanced at the foreman and grinned. He liked Levi's easy-going drawl, and the cynical dryness in his voice when he spoke.

The foreman's .45, Pasco noticed, rested in a well-oiled cutaway holster, slung low on his right thigh and tied to his leg with a leather thong— the trademark of professional gunmen. Pasco realized that all the Crazy Creek riders seemed to have been cut from the same pattern—quiet, quick-eyed men. Not much like the common run of cowhands. He thought wryly: you ought to feel right at home here. The place for a hardcase is with a hardcase crew, isn't it?

Pasco turned his own horse into the corral for feeding, and the wrangler, on Levi's order, cut out a tall bay gelding for him. Most of the men were saddled now, waiting only for Hornsby's orders to move out.

Pasco swung up to his saddle and sat for a moment, staring out at the silver-edged darkness. At another time he would have been impressed with the quiet beauty of the prairie night. But not now. Over there to the north there were armed men waiting for them.

Across the lot, Hornsby, still flanked by his two-man bodyguard, was taking up his position in front of his army. When the shooting starts, Pasco thought dimly, I wonder how long he'll stay in front like that? Levi, almost as though he had been reading Pasco's thoughts, gave him a grin.

"You ready over there, Carl?" the rancher called.

"Ready."

In imitation of a cavalry commander, Hornsby lifted an arm and swung it forward. Levi spat at the ground, then nudged his horse, and he and Pasco swung in with the other riders. They rode out of the ranch yard, around the barns toward the north.

If the men were thinking any special thoughts they kept them silent. They were hired to fight, and now they were going to earn their money—a hardcase's life was as simple as that—as long as it lasted.

While Hornsby led his small band across the darkened flatlands, Levi and Pasco fell back to the rear and rode quietly in the dusty drag.

"How many men do you expect Otto to have at the dam?" Pasco said finally.

"A dozen, at least, and probably more, depending on how many riders Hilderbrand is putting in the battle."

The sense of unreality seized Pasco again. A million acres of grass, and three men fighting over it—but it was real enough for the men riding in grim silence up ahead of them. It was real enough for other quiet men waiting at the dam. And Pasco only had to remember that Otto was up there ahead somewhere, waiting. That was the thing that mattered.

After a while Hornsby called back to his foreman, and Levi pushed his horse up to the head of the band, motioning for Pasco to come with him. "There's the creek over there," the rancher said, motioning toward a denser darkness over to his right, where willows and salt cedar clustered along the banks of the stream.

"It's the creek," Levi said, "but we won't be seeing the dam for several minutes yet."

The rancher was losing his early bravado. The night was cool, but his forehead seemed to be damp, as he dabbed at it with a large bandanna. "Just the same, there's no use taking chances on an ambush. I want you to take some scouts, Carl, and go up ahead. If it looks all right, I'll bring up the rest of the boys."

The foreman shrugged. "Whatever you say. But

if we stay away from the creek I don't expect we'll see an ambush."

Turning his horse, he called, "Martin! Stoneridge! Cut out from the bunch; we're going up ahead."

Pasco said, "I'd like to go, if you don't mind."

Another shrug from the foreman. "If you're that anxious for battle, it's all right with me." Martin and Stoneridge rode to the front and Levi said, "Spread out and we'll screen ahead as far as the creek bend below the dam." The horsemen, without a word, wheeled and rode into the darkness.

The foreman would have made a good cavalry officer, Pasco thought—and he probably had been one, once.

Levi took the right flank and Martin the left, with Stoneridge and Pasco forming the center line. They rode slowly for perhaps five minutes, until they could see the blurred shapes of scrubby growth along the creek banks.

"This's far enough," Levi called softly.

The words were hardly spoken when a rifle cracked open the night's silence. Not waiting for orders, the four horsemen scattered and Levi yelled: "It's just a lookout. Martin, you go back and tell Silas he can come on up—if he still wants to."

The rifle spoke again, sharply, spitting a bright stream of fire, and then was silent. Pasco had already dismounted, leading his horse through the brush and into the shallow gully which was Crazy Creek. He kept his .45 holstered, for there was no sense wasting cartridges in the darkness. And besides, the lookout was gone by now.

Two more horsemen came crashing into the undergrowth and Pasco said, "Over here." Levi and Stoneridge hitched their horses to willow branches and stumbled along the creek bank to where Pasco was waiting.

"See anything?" Levi asked.

"Just what you saw. The lookout has already pulled out, I think. Is the dam close to here?"

The foreman hunkered down, his back against the damp clay bank, and methodically began fishing for the makings of a cigarette. "Maybe four hundred yards up the creek. No more. I guess what we ought to do is move on up the creek," he said, "and see if we can find out how many there are and where they're hiding. I can't say I'm crazy about the job, though."

Pasco would have taken the job gladly, if he had been sure that he would find Otto. But he said nothing, and then they heard sounds of horses in the darkness and Levi's match flared and was snuffed out as he lighted his cigarette. "Maybe we'd better wait and see what Silas aims to do." The other rider, Stoneridge, laughed dryly.

Levi roused himself as the other horseman

began skittering noisily into the draw. "What was the shooting about?" Hornsby wanted to know.

"The lookout letting the others know we're here," Levi said.

Nervously, Hornsby began wiping his forehead again. After a pause he said, "Then we'll go on up the creek on foot, I guess."

The foreman almost laughed. "I guess it'll save some horses from being shot. Is the dynamite coming up?"

"On a buckboard. It ought to be up pretty soon." The other riders left their horses at the lower end of the draw and came up the creek bed crashing noisily through the brush.

Levi hitched at his cartridge belt. "I guess there's not much sense in being quiet. We're not likely to surprise anybody tonight."

Pasco, standing to one side, could almost see the color rushing to the rancher's face, even in the darkness. He looked as if he wanted to say something, but didn't know just what would be the right thing. "Well," he said at last, "we might as well go."

"Up the creek?" Levi asked.

"It's better than trying to reach the dam across open country."

"It would be better for an ambush, too, in case Otto has been thinking along that line."

Hornsby made a startled, grunting sound, then seemed to notice Pasco for the first time. "Pasco, you go on ahead, and if anything goes wrong, fire three shots. The rest of us will come on behind you."

At another time, Hornsby's playing the part of a commanding officer might have been humorous, but now the humor of the situation escaped even Carl Levi. The foreman glanced at Pasco, then leveled his gaze at the rancher. "I'm still drawing fighting pay," he said shortly. "I'll take the job."

Pasco's estimate of the foreman was rising. "I'll go with you," he said, and the foreman's eyebrows came together in a brief scowl.

"Suit yourself."

It took them almost five minutes to cover a hundred yards in the tangled brush and sloppy creek bottom. There was no easy way to do it. Up ahead Otto's men were almost certain to be hiding behind some kind of makeshift fortifications guarding the open approaches to the dam. But there was no way of knowing whether he had men guarding the creek bed itself. It was dirty, monotonously slow work, picking their way through the mud and brush, on their hands and knees most of the time. At last Levi stopped, and Pasco moved up alongside him.

"You see anything?"

Levi grunted. "I feel like a damned fool. If Otto sits quiet and lets us slip in the back door and blow up his dam, he's a bigger fool than I figured him to be."

There was nothing to say to that. Otto would be called many things, but fool wasn't one of them. Pasco eased forward a few paces and rested against the clay bank. "If we run into the ambush you expect, what do we do then?"

"Run like hell, most likely. We can't expect any help from Hornsby." He pulled his hat down on his forehead and began inching forward. "Maybe this is where we start earning our fighting pay."

Now they moved even more cautiously as they got closer to the dam. Back behind them they could hear the uneasy stirring of the Crazy Creek horses, but as they moved farther away it vanished altogether.

Levi paused for a moment, listening. His hands and knees were slimy with mud; there was mud on his face where he had wiped it on the sleeve of his shirt. "I expected to hear something before now. The dam isn't far away, we'll be able to see it as soon as we round this next bend."

They began moving again. As they crawled, Pasco could hear Levi cursing, almost silently, and he kept it up until they reached the bend. The dam was up ahead, dark, quiet, with no sign of life around it.

Pasco found that he was dragging huge gulps of air into his lungs. Levi stood up on his knees, like an ungainly bear. "Well, there it is." He wiped his long nose on his shirt sleeve. "And I can't say that I like it. Something should have happened before now."

But nothing happened. Pasco had the feeling that he was being watched. Otto and his men were up there somewhere. It was too much to hope that he would show his hole card until he knew how the hand was going.

Levi began moving backwards, still on his hands and knees. "Let's get out of here. Fighting pay is fine, but it doesn't cover suicide."

"You think Otto's up there?"

"Somebody's up there. I can't see them, but there are some things a man knows without having to see."

Going back was even more tortuous than coming forward had been. Pasco glanced at Levi and grinned thinly.

They seemed to travel miles instead of yards, but at last they began to hear the movements of horses and men far down the gully. "Well, at least they're still there," Levi grunted. Then he stood up, cutting the caked mud from the front of his shirt.

They heard Hornsby call: "That you, Carl? Pasco?"

"We may not look it, but it's us all right," the foreman said. The two men walked up to the silent cluster of Crazy Creek riders.

"Did you get to the dam?" Hornsby said.

"We got close enough to see the dam, but that's all. Otto's got his men out of sight, but I think they saw us."

"How do you know, if you didn't see anything?"

"I don't know. I've just got the feeling that, for the last several minutes, I've been watched over a dozen sets of gunsights. Call it a hunch, if you want to."

"Nonsense," Hornsby snorted. "If they had seen you, they'd have opened fire. The thing to do is go right up the creek and take the dam. Otto's figuring us to charge his position from the south. We'll fool him."

Pasco spoke for the first time. "They know what we're up to, all right."

The rancher turned and glared pettishly. "Did you see them?"

"No. But they're there."

Hornsby laughed, but the sound was strained. "I thought I'd hired on men, not children who get scared by their own shadows. I tell you they don't know I've got the crew within two miles of their dam. We'll go straight up the creek, like I said."

That ended it, as far as Hornsby was concerned, and it didn't make any difference to Pasco. Charging across the open would be just as dangerous, probably, unless Otto was at this moment organizing his men for an all-out ambush.

Pasco and the foreman watched the rancher give his pompous orders. The buckboard bearing the blasting powder was waiting farther down the stream, and now Hornsby sent men down to bring it up.

When everything was ready, Hornsby ordered the men forward.

It was impossible for even one man to move silently along the sloppy creek bottom—with a dozen and more men, the noise seemed almost deafening in the narrow confines of the draw. Pasco drew his .45 and checked it as well as he could in the darkness. Levi, he noticed, was doing the same. Hornsby, confident now that he was outsmarting both Otto and Hilderbrand, passed the word back to have the dynamite ready.

Then—as suddenly as if the sky had fallen—a dozen guns exploded on top of them.

Chapter Eight

Dimly, Pasco remembered hearing the rancher scream, but he didn't stop to see if he had been hit. With the other men, Pasco dived for the brush along the creek banks, slopping through the mud as he fumbled for his revolver. The gully was suddenly and incredibly alight with flashing guns; the noise was like sudden thunderclaps as Pasco dived into the mud under the acrid-smelling branches of a cedar.

The men were yelling, scrambling, running in every direction. Yet, at that moment, Pasco felt more alone than he had ever been before. He found himself evaluating the situation, guessing at what must have happened. One thing was clear; the ambush had been planned. It was no accident. That was proof enough that his and Levi's scouting expedition had been less than successful. Otto must have drawn all his men from the dam.

That was as far as Pasco got with his thinking. A bullet ripped viciously through the branches of the cedar and slammed into the mud near his head. Pasco lurched forward, his .45 in his hand. He held his fire and yelled for the men behind him to climb the creek bank. The most important thing at that moment was getting out of that gully. Then, even as he yelled, he stumbled across something soft and went crashing down to his knees.

There was a soft, almost unrecognizable sound. "Pasco?"

Pasco realized that he had fallen over a man. The foreman.

"Get out of here. Get out of the gully before everybody's killed." The words were drawn tight, and, although Pasco could not see his face, he knew that Levi's voice was coming through pain-clenched teeth. Quickly, Pasco rolled the foreman over, got his shoulder under Levi's body and lifted. It was dead weight. Pasco stumbled, went down to one knee. Immediately, he lifted himself again and began clawing at the loose clay of the steep bank.

In his exertion he felt sweat beading on his forehead and neck, running in cold trickles across his face and shoulders. In some corner of his mind Pasco was vaguely aware of the crash and fire of guns, but he could think of only one thing at that moment—getting out of the creek bed. Straining, he reached high, grasping a slippery willow trunk and, inch by inch, he worked himself up until he had reached the top of the bank.

He let the foreman roll from his shoulders, and for a moment Pasco lay exhausted, his face pressed to the damp grass, pulling long draughts of air into his lungs. Levi didn't move, and finally

Pasco realized that the foreman was dead—had been dead all through the desperate struggle to the top of the bank.

He lay there for what seemed hours, listening to the crashing of guns.

Over the steady bombardment, men were yelling. Some of them were Otto's, some Hornsby's and probably some of Hilderbrand's, too. Maybe in another second some of them would be dead. Fighting pay didn't seem like so much when you saw the way the foreman had had to earn his.

The thoughts rambled senselessly in Pasco's mind as he strove to pull more air into his lungs, to put out the fire. He raised himself to his hands and knees and saw that other members of Hornsby's crew were fighting their way up the side of the creek bank.

Pasco stood up and shouted. "Hornsby, bring your men up here!"

There was no answer from below except for the confused firing and shouting. Other guns opened up farther up the creek and Pasco dropped to his knees again as bullets ripped into the ground beside him. He cupped his hands and yelled again.

"Hornsby!"

There was no answer.

Across the creek was the confused sound of movement, the sound of men racing through the brush toward the lower end of the draw. Pasco knew what that meant. Otto was sending his men down to cut off Hornsby's retreat—if that was what Hornsby meant to do. Otto meant to make it a clean, clear-cut victory, so overwhelming that it would stamp him for all time as the boss of the Panhandle.

For a moment Pasco felt something for Otto that neared admiration. Such determination to get what he wanted amounted to a kind of virtue in this country. If Otto had been a stranger, if he had been anybody besides the man he really was—The thought ended abruptly. A voice—a hoarse bellowing voice from the other side of the creek—sounded over the noise of the shooting.

"On the other side! They're coming up the other bank!"

It was Otto's voice. For a moment, Pasco was motionless; he let himself enjoy the cruel satisfaction that comes with closed combat with a hated enemy. For Pasco, there were only two people there that mattered—Otto Keller and himself.

The moment of satisfaction ended suddenly as another bullet slashed into the ground beside him. Someone had spotted him. The Rocker-O men up closer to the dam, probably, but there wasn't time to wonder about it. A hand appeared over the edge of the bank, then a head, and Pasco recognized the man as one of Hornsby's two bodyguards.

The rider pulled himself up the bank and then lurched over on the ledge, gasping for air. Pasco knelt beside him.

"Is Hornsby down there?"

"Lord knows. The last I seen of him he was headed toward the lower end of the creek."

"He can't get out that way. Otto's sent men down there to cut us off."

The rider spat, lifted himself to his knees. "I know it. But there's no stopping Silas when he's scared." He grinned fleetingly. "Not that I wasn't scared, too."

If Hornsby ran now, Otto would never let him stop; he'd run that Crazy Creek rancher clear out of Texas. Pasco found himself punching the used cartridges out of his .45 and replacing them with new rounds from his belt. Well, he thought grimly, if I've got anything to say about it, Hornsby's not running. This is one fight that Otto's not going to win, if I can help it.

"Is that Levi?" the man asked, glancing at the still figure of the foreman.

"He's dead," Pasco said shortly. "And a lot more of us will be, if we don't make a stand. You stay here and get the men to form behind that pile of driftwood."

"Where're you going?"

"Back into the creek bed and see if I can find Hornsby."

His .45 in his hand, Pasco slid over the edge

and dropped back into the brush and mud of the creek bottom. Most of the Crazy Creek riders had taken up what protection they could find behind the flimsy willows and cedars, and were firing blindly into the darkness. "Get out of this creek bed!" Pasco heard himself bellowing angrily. "Get up on the bank where we can make a stand!"

Thrashing through the tangle of brush, he almost stumbled over one of the Crazy Creek riders. "Have you seen Hornsby?"

"He's down below somewhere."

Pasco started the man climbing the steep clay banks, sending others after him, as he floundered through the muddy creek bottom. The shooting was slacking off now as Otto shifted his men to meet the new threat. Pasco stood grimly, ankle-deep in mud, peering vainly into the darkness.

"Hornsby!"

This time an answer came weakly from the far end of the draw.

"Is that you, Pasco?"

Pasco saw the rancher then, crouched low behind a lacy willow. "We can't get out," Hornsby whimpered. "They've got us cut off!"

Pasco knelt beside him for a moment, getting his breath. "We can make a stand up above. I've got the men headed in that direction. Your foreman's dead. He got it in that first volley."

Hornsby didn't seem to hear. He was hopelessly defeated, and without any idea of what to do about it. Pasco suddenly lost all patience, as his anger turned to disgust. "Get up, damn it! I tell you we've got to get out of this gully and make a stand, or none of us will get out alive. Do you know where the dynamite is?"

Dumbly, the rancher shook his head. Another of their men came crashing toward them from the lower end of the gully, a bulging burlap sack slung over his shoulder. He dropped down by Hornsby and placed the bag on the ground with elaborate care.

"Here's your dynamite. I can't see that it's goin' to do much good, though."

"I'll take it," Pasco said. "You gather up the rest of the riders. We're making a stand up above."

The man nodded, and after a moment he went stumbling on up the creek. It didn't strike Pasco as unusual that he had suddenly begun to give orders, or that the men were taking them. But Hornsby was looking at him curiously. His eyes held a respect that Pasco hadn't noticed before.

"Levi—" Hornsby said finally. "He's dead?"

Pasco nodded shortly, pulling the rancher roughly to his feet. "And so will we be, if we don't get out of here."

"Just a minute." He grasped Pasco's shoulder and held tightly for a moment, making his decision quickly. "You're the new foreman," he said, after a pause of a few seconds. "It'll go on the books that way tomorrow. If you can get us out of this."

Pasco grinned tightly. A new man rising from rider to foreman in the space of a few hours. He wasn't sure how the rest of the riders were going to take the news, but that was of little importance now. And anyway, Hornsby might change his mind in the light of day, if he lived to see it.

Pasco half led and half pulled the rancher out of the creek bottom. They were the last ones to leave, as far as Pasco could tell. The shooting was beginning again up above, but that seemed unimportant until they reached the top of the bank and got their breath.

"You—" The rancher was blowing hard. "You say we can make a stand up here?"

"There's a place up ahead." Hornsby was on his own now. The dynamite had been left behind in the draw, where Pasco hoped he could find it if the chance came to use it. Now he crouched low, his revolver in his hand, running a zigzag course toward the driftwood fortress. He didn't look back to see if Hornsby was following.

There were a dozen men gathered behind the piles of driftwood, and a few more flanked out from the creek, behind rocks, pouring their fire in the direction of the dam. Pasco went down to one knee beside the man he recognized again as Hornsby's side man. The man grunted, peering over the sights of his .45.

"How does it look?" Pasco asked.

"Better than the creek bottom. It looks like we've got a stand-off here—for a while, anyway. Until Otto brings up reinforcements."

Pasco didn't mean to wait that long. Glancing along the length of the drift pile, he saw some of the Crazy Creek riders pulling back from their positions at the breastworks. Pasco stood up and yelled, "Get back! Keep firing at the dam!"

But he saw that his shouting would do no good. With the foreman dead, the men were losing heart for the fight. They wanted to get back to their horses and save themselves before Otto's reinforcements came up.

Pasco felt a savage, unreasonable anger tug at him. He crouched low, running toward the retreating men. A gutless few could steal his victory over Otto, and that he would not have! He flung himself at one of the startled men and the rider staggered back before the onslaught. Pasco swung savagely with his fist and heard the man grunt in surprise and hurt. Pasco shot his fist in again, unmindful of the firing from the dam, and the amazed rider fell sprawling.

Standing furiously over the fallen rider, Pasco leveled his .45 at the others, and his voice turned cold and hard.

"If there's any man here not drawing fighting pay, he can go. The others are going to stay until I give the word to pull out. Is that clear?"

Surprised, Pasco heard Hornsby's voice calling from the drift pile. "Do as he says! He's taking Levi's place with the crew."

The men hesitated for a moment. They showed no fear of Hornsby, but they were reluctant to face Pasco's savagery. Pasco began moving forward, only vaguely aware of the bullets striking heavily about them. He gestured with his gun to one of the men. "Do you draw fighting pay?"

An angry grunt was the only answer.

"Then get back with the others!"

The revolt was broken as suddenly as it had begun.

One of the men went down to a crouch and jogged doggedly back to his position. After a brief moment, the others did the same. Pasco gave himself an instant to let his anger cool, and then he turned and went back to the brush pile where Hornsby was waiting.

Glancing at him nervously, the rancher said, "That was a fool thing to do. We've got to pull out of here sometime, Pasco, and it might as well be now."

"You want the dam dynamited, don't you?"

"You know what happened to us down in the creek. We'll never have a chance to reach that dam again."

Hornsby was fighting himself as hard as he was fighting Otto. Pasco glanced back at the creek.

"Just keep your men firing. Keep Otto's attention directed at this brush pile."

He didn't give the rancher time to ask questions. He fired once in the direction of the dam, and then began melting back into the deeper darkness. Blowing the dam was a one-man job. It should have been done this way the first time.

He found the dynamite where he had left it in the creek bed, beneath the drooping branches of a willow. The steady firing up above seemed far away and unimportant now, as Pasco laid out the dynamite and formed it into two packets of six sticks each. The length of fuse he stuffed into his pants pocket, along with half a dozen sulphur matches.

Ignoring the rattle of revolver and carbine fire, he began making his way up the creek. There was no need for silence this time. An army could have crashed its way through the gully, unheard over the noise of the battle. Still it was necessary to stay in the deeper shadows as much as possible, and Pasco took his time.

For a moment he allowed himself a small, grim smile when he imagined how old Otto's face would look as the dam went up in thunder. But that small pleasure was short-lived. There would be time to think of Otto later.

He reached the bend in the creek where he and Levi had turned back on their scouting expedition. Up ahead was the hulking shape of the dam, but Otto seemed to have his men concentrated on the other side. That was good. Pasco felt his way carefully now, cautious as he crawled, keeping the fuse and dynamite bundles dry. He moved forward, and now he could see the dam clearly. He could see that it was constructed of logs and brush and filled in with dirt. It was a makeshift dam, but very solid. It was Otto's, and Otto always did things right.

He could hear the Rocker-O firing now, almost on top of him, it seemed. Pasco paused for what seemed a long while, half expecting the firing to change direction suddenly and rain its full fury down into the creek again.

Nothing happened. Sticking to the shadows, he began crawling again.

At last he reached the base of the dam. Ankle-deep in mud, covered in slime, he could hear the Rocker-O riders cursing as they kept up the steady barrage aimed at the drift pile. He could hear Otto shouting hoarsely, his voice sounding flat and harsh, even above the racket.

Methodically now, without emotion, Pasco began working with his hands, gouging deep holes back into the dam as far as he could reach. When the holes were completed, he fixed the fuses and shoved the dynamite bundles all the way in, packing them solidly with wet clay from the creek bed. The fuses must be short. That was important. If the flash of the match was seen, or the spewing of the fuse, he didn't want to give Otto a chance to stop the explosion.

He bruised the ends of the fuses with his fingers, fraying them slightly. Then in the brief, bluish flare of the sulphur match, he smiled. Then Pasco lurched up and began crashing down the creek bed, away from the dam.

The explosion tore an angry gash in the night. The shock of it struck Pasco like a giant hand, sending him sprawling as the great shower of splintered wood and dirt began raining down. Pasco picked himself up and stumbled on. The last thing he remembered thinking was: that's only the first payment, Otto! And then he felt a shocking hurt, hitting him from behind. He stumbled once, then fell forward into blackness.

Chapter Nine

Pasco awakened with bright sun in his face, far away from the place where the battle had been. There was the clean smell of horses and new hay, and instinctively Pasco knew that he was in a barn.

He became aware of the woman-sound of rustling taffeta. Opening his eyes, he stared blankly up at Peg Manning, who was kneeling beside him.

"Peg? For a minute there I thought I was seeing things."

She didn't smile. The only expression in her eyes was one of weariness. Pasco lurched up on one elbow, wincing at the hammering in his head.

"You'd better lie down," Peg said flatly. "You're not hurt badly, but you need to rest."

"Where am I, anyway? And what are you doing here, Peg?"

She dipped a white cloth into a pan of cool water, then wrung it out and handed it to Pasco. "Put this on your head for a few minutes and you'll feel better. You're in Silas Hornsby's barn now, along with three others who were hurt last night, not counting Carl Levi. After the fight at the dam, Silas sent into Messina for Doc Fuller. I came along as a nurse. You were hit by a piece of timber from the explosion," Peg said.

At last he said, "Did Silas's men come out all right?"

He opened his eyes and she was smiling at him with a strange coldness, completely without humor. "Everything's fine," she said dryly. "The dam is destroyed. One Crazy Creek man is dead and four more are hurt. We don't know yet how many of Otto Keller's men were killed or hurt in the explosion. Doc Fuller is over there now, seeing what he can do."

She stood abruptly, and Pasco saw that three other men were laid out on straw pallets on either side of the barn door. One was smoking a cigarette, his leg in splints. The others seemed to be sleeping.

Without giving him another glance, Peg Manning picked up her bandages and water and walked out of the barn, as stiff and erect as an arrow.

Then he heard the sound of horses coming slowly from the north. With an effort, Pasco pushed himself to a sitting position, only half listening to the riders' voices as they turned their horses into the corral. The brilliant sun beat like hammers at his eyeballs and, for a moment, Pasco covered his face with his hands, waiting for the sudden sickness to pass.

Determinedly, Pasco pushed himself to his knees, then to his feet. Recognizing Hornsby's voice, Pasco made his way weakly to the doorway. He saw that the rancher was not alone.

Pasco stared blankly for a moment, still too sick to feel surprised. Marshal Bunt Wallace was striding stiffly beside Hornsby, his big face completely expressionless, his eyes cold. At Wallace's side there was a slight, dapper little man decked out immaculately in broadcloth and boiled linen. He looked ridiculous with the huge double-action .45 he wore strapped around his middle.

The Crazy Creek owner seemed to be in fine spirits. His usually flaccid face now creased in smiles as he saw Pasco.

"Ah," the rancher said, "I see you're up. How's the head?"

Pasco shrugged. He was beginning to feel better. "What have you heard from Otto?"

Hornsby laughed. "We beat Otto last night—or rather you did, Pasco. And I'm not forgetting it. I've got the boys staked out up north where the creek forks."

"Isn't that Otto's land?"

"That's why I sent the boys up there. If Otto tries to dam the creek on us again, we'll do the same to him. Not that I think he'll do it. After that explosion, Otto's crew is scattered all over Messina County."

Hornsby was highly pleased with this new idea of his, but Pasco doubted that beating Otto was going to be that simple. The rancher went on, "I want you to meet an old friend of mine. Sheriff Pat St. John." He laughed again briefly. "I've been telling Pat how you took care of that dam last night. The sheriff came up from Messina to make sure Otto doesn't try a thing like that again."

Pasco took St. John's hand briefly, understanding immediately why there was so little respect for law and order in Messina County.

The sheriff was a pallid, timid little politician of a man, and at this moment he looked flustered and worried. He wiped his face with a white handkerchief which he took from the breast pocket of his broadcloth coat. "Now, Silas, you haven't got it exactly right. I've already got Otto's promise that he won't dam the creek again, and I want you to promise that you'll pull your men away from the Forks."

Hornsby said heartily, "Of course, Sheriff. You know I never wanted any trouble with Otto or Hilderbrand. There'll be no more range war. You can depend on it. That is, unless the Rocker-O and the Double-O Star want to start it again."

The little sheriff looked relieved, as though he actually believed Hornsby meant what he said.

Bunt Wallace said: "I think I'll stay around for a while, Sheriff, and see what I can find."

"Sure, sure," the little man said absently. "I've already spoken to Keller. He's expecting you."

Bunt Wallace didn't move as Hornsby and the

sheriff started back toward the ranch headquarters building. Finally he reached for his makings and began rolling a thin cigarette. As he did so, Pasco had the feeling that he had seen the marshal before somewhere. Wallace glanced at him as he struck a match on his thumbnail.

"I hear you've got to be foreman already," he said flatly.

"That's what Hornsby tells me. Aren't you stretching your territory a little these days, Marshal?"

Wallace grinned thinly. "Not exactly. I'm still looking for that bushwhacker that took a shot at you back at Messina. I had the blacksmith take a look at the shoe marks where he found the cartridge cases—he claims the shoeing job wasn't done by him, nor by anybody else in this country. Otto, Hilderbrand, and Hornsby seem to be the only ones around here hiring riders from other territories, so I thought I'd have a look."

"Help yourself," Pasco said shortly. "But I told you who was responsible for the bushwhacking. I'll get him myself, before it's over."

The marshal never lost his smile, but the bitterness behind his eyes was unmistakable. He said suddenly, with a harshness that surprised Pasco: "If you'd been smart, you'd have pulled out of the county, the way I warned you. But your kind is never smart." Then he turned abruptly on his heel and walked away.

Pasco stared blankly for a moment, wondering what had gotten into the marshal.

It was near noon that day when Pasco rigged up his roan and started the long ride toward the Forks. He had eaten and he had had time to shave and clean up, and his head had cleared and no longer hurt so much. He should have felt good. He was drawing a foreman's wage now on top of his regular fighting pay, and he had proven to himself and to Hornsby that he could control the men. More important, he had taken the first round from Otto—but the sense of satisfaction was missing.

For a moment he had the uneasy feeling that Peg Manning had something to do with it, but that didn't make much sense. It made no difference to him what a Messina dressmaker thought or said. There was another thing, too, that nagged at the back of his mind. For some reason he felt that he would be more at ease if he could get Marshal Bunt Wallace pegged in his memory.

The noonday sun beat down on the flatland, and as Pasco rode he gazed idly at the scattered Crazy Creek herds gathered at the stream. At least he had the satisfaction of knowing that even if he did nothing else for Hornsby, he had already earned his foreman's wage. For, if the dam had stood, part of those cattle would be near to dying by now.

The thought carried itself logically on from there. If Hornsby's men could hold the Forks, if they could somehow dam off the creek and shut off Otto's water without cutting off their own supply—

He was not particularly surprised to see a rider move out of the willows along the creek bank and come toward him. The distance was too great to be sure who the rider was, but Pasco guessed it was one of Hornsby's men. Probably a line rider making sure that the herds didn't move toward Otto's range.

Suddenly Pasco came erect in his saddle. He stared for a moment as the rider grew nearer, realizing that it wasn't a man at all. His insides seemed to go empty as he stared at her, and he knew instinctively, even before he could see her face, that it was Myra.

As she came on, Pasco shook his head savagely, as a sleeper would try to shake off an unwanted dream.

Myra was no dream, though. When she was near enough, she said quietly, "You came back, John. At last you came back."

Pasco sat staring at her, amazed at how little she had changed in five years.

She rode a sleek, high-strung bay thoroughbred with expertness. Smiling, she reined her horse down alongside Pasco. "Don't you remember me, John?"

"What are you doing here on Hornsby's range?" he asked, finally.

She smiled again, a slow smile so warm that it melted a part of the hard core inside him. "I expected you to be pleased that I came."

"In five years," he said, "a man's apt to change."

But she shook her head. "Five years, five days, five hours—they're all the same to us. Or to me, anyway."

"Why?" Pasco heard himself saying flatly.

Her smile was suddenly gone. "Because I still love you, John. Nothing will ever change that."

"A little thing like love didn't stop you from marrying Otto," he said bitterly.

She sat for a moment in silence, hardly seeming to breathe. She whispered, "I'm sorry, John." Then she reined the bay around and rode back toward the creek.

Pasco sat stunned for a moment, aware that his tightly clenched teeth had set up a nervous quivering in the muscles of his jaw. After all, Myra, he thought savagely, it's been five years. A man changes, but he doesn't forget. I haven't forgotten the letters you didn't write, the explanations you didn't make. And I haven't forgotten that you're married to Otto.

He called, "Myra!"

She rode on without looking back.

Putting iron to his roan, he spurted forward to overtake her.

The thoroughbred neither slacked nor speeded

its pace. As Pasco drew alongside he leaned forward and grabbed the bay's bridle reins, pulling the animal down to a walk. Myra still said nothing, refusing to look at him. They rode on for a few more yards to the edge of the creek bank where the willows made cool, rattling sounds in the afternoon, and Pasco suddenly blurted:

"Myra, why did you come here?"

She offered no resistance when Pasco dropped down from the saddle, still holding the bay's reins. Trying to keep his voice calm, he said: "You rode all the way from Otto's place to say something. You might as well say it."

Still not looking at him, she said, "It doesn't matter now."

Pasco's anger seemed to melt, looking at her. Her hair still had life, catching the fire of the sun now. Her eyes were still clear, her skin still as fresh and perfectly tinted as delicate china. What was it she had said: Five years . . . five days . . . five hours. It made no difference—to her.

She looked down at him then, and at that moment nothing seemed to matter except that the two of them were together. Pasco forgot she was now Otto's wife as he lifted his arms and helped her down from the saddle.

"John." She made a small choking sound as Pasco took her in his arms and held her close against him. "You're back, John. That's all that matters. Nothing else is important."

"No, I guess not."

He could feel her smiling, her face pressed to his shoulder. "Why did you come back, John? Was it because of me or Otto?"

"I thought it was Otto. But I guess it was some of both." There was a question that had to be asked, and it might as well be now. He released her on the pretence of bringing back his straying roan. When he came back to the creek bank he began rolling a cigarette to give his hands something to do. Not looking at her, he said, "Myra . . ." But before he could go any further she was in his arms again, clinging to him.

"I know what you're going to say, but don't talk about it now. Not right this minute." Then, her face pressed against his shoulder, she said, "But we can't overlook it, can we?" She tried a smile that didn't quite come off. "You've got a right to know why I married Otto. I'll tell you."

And in a slow, halting way, which was not like Myra at all, she went on:

"Can you understand what it's like to be all by yourself, to be alone and unhappy, and sometimes frightened? That's the way it was with me, John, after they sent you away. For four years, and longer, I waited. When you got out of Huntsville, I thought you'd come back. I thought we could begin again and make new plans, make a new life. But you didn't come back. Not until it was too late. I waited a long time, John, and finally

128

there was no fight and no hope left in me. You can't blame me for that, can you?"

She spoke softly, almost to herself, it seemed.

"And Otto was always there. Wherever I looked, Otto would be there. He offered me the world," she said, looking directly at Pasco, "if I would marry him. He built a new Rocker-O headquarters house just for me. He had new furniture shipped all the way from Kansas City. He had carpets and mirrors and pictures sent from St. Louis. He got my silverware and china and jewelry in New Orleans. He had dresses sent from Chicago. All those things he did for me, and many more. And you weren't here. I didn't know if you'd ever come back. I didn't even know if you wanted to see me again."

Those aren't reasons, Myra, Pasco thought. They're excuses. But he said small, meaningless things, made clumsy attempts to comfort her, to reassure her, and all the time he knew it was hopeless.

Myra glanced up at him and she could see the things that were working in his mind. Before Pasco could speak, she said, "Don't talk now, John, not for a little while." Then, after a moment, she said, "John, is it true that Silas Hornsby has made you foreman?"

The question surprised Pasco, until he remembered that Doc Fuller must have taken the news to the Rocker-O when he visited there that morning. Pasco nodded briefly, and Myra smiled and seemed pleased.

"John, you *have* changed. You're bigger, you're stronger than you were before. You're the kind of man I knew you would be some day."

Pasco looked down at her. She was still as selfish as a beautiful child.

"Yes," she said thoughtfully, still smiling, "you're strong now. Stronger than my father, maybe even stronger than Otto." She nodded her head eagerly. "You came back to Messina to ruin Otto, didn't you? To kill him, maybe. You can do it now, John; I know you can."

Pasco thought wryly, maybe I have changed, but you haven't, Myra. He allowed himself a thin smile. "If my aim is to kill your husband, it doesn't seem to bother you."

Her smile vanished. "I hate him!" she hissed. "I can't stand to look at him. My flesh crawls when he touches me."

"But you married him!"

"I tried to explain that, but—" She closed her eyes and he could feel her shudder. "Oh, John, I didn't know it would be like this!"

"It's no use, Myra."

Again she saw what he was thinking and tried to stop him. "Don't talk. Just hold me for a moment; hold me close."

It isn't a pretty picture, Pasco thought, when a man stands back and finally has a look at himself and sees himself for the fool he really is. He touched her hair, gently, in the way a man might try to comfort a child. Suddenly he broke away from her and walked stiffly toward his waiting horse.

"John!"

In one quick movement, Pasco hit the stirrup and swung up to the saddle. He didn't dare look at her. Reining around roughly, he rode away from the creek as she called to him again.

"I'll be here tomorrow, John. I'll be waiting!"

His impulse was to turn and go back to her. He wanted to hold her again. He wanted to hear her tell him how much she loved him. He wanted to hear again how much she hated Otto.

He rode north, without looking back. The book had been closed five years ago, and there was no opening it now, no matter how much he wanted to. When I fight Otto, he thought grimly, I'll fight him for my own reasons. I'll kill him if I can— and that will be because of my own reasons. Not yours, Myra.

Chapter Ten

By the time Pasco reached the Forks, he pretended to himself that Myra was forgotten. And he set himself to making preparations for the attack that he knew Otto would soon be throwing at them. Crazy Creek was in reality a small branch of the Canadian River, which rambled east to west across the upper part of the Panhandle. The creek meandered crazily north to south through most of Messina County, finally joining with the Muleshoe, which played out eventually in the parched flatlands to the east.

But it was the southern part of the creek that interested Pasco now. It branched off several times between the Canadian and the northern tip of the county, and in most cases the branches soon played out in the semidesert. There was only one major fork that ran water the year around, and that was on the land that Otto claimed for his north range. One prong wandered deep into Hornsby's property, and the other prong split Otto's holdings down the middle.

Pasco picked up the trace of Hornsby's riders and followed it to the north. He was on Otto's property now, and far to the east he could see small clusters of the Rocker-O herds scattered across the prairie. Before long Pasco could see the open triangle of the Forks, three thin lines of green marching across the drab flatland. Then he began hearing the cracks of rifles.

He guessed that the Forks hadn't turned out to be so easy to hold as Hornsby had first figured.

Pasco changed his course, swinging far to the west in a long arc until he reached the creek, and then he rode down toward the Forks. In a shallow draw he saw several horses bearing the Crazy Creek brand, and as he rode toward them a man came out of the brush, carrying a short carbine at the ready. The man grunted, then spat as he recognized Pasco.

"You're the new ramrod, I guess."

Pasco nodded. "What's going on down below?"

The wrangler slipped a piece of tobacco into his mouth and took a bite. "Old Hilderbrand must have joined forces with Otto last night or this morning. Anyway, they came up the creek about two hours ago and made things hot for us at the Forks. We moved back here, and ever since we've just been taking pot shots at each other, neither side doing much damage."

Being forced away from the Forks was enough damage, Pasco thought. But he only nodded and climbed stiffly out of the saddle. He turned the horse over to the wrangler and began making his way south along the creek bank.

The firing was closer now, but it was sporadic and had a vaguely apathetic sound, as though no malice were intended. Then Pasco saw a group of men below him, sitting with their backs against the sloped creek bank. They were talking lazily, chewing, spitting, paying little attention to the firing farther down the creek.

With a grunt of impatience, Pasco vaulted over the edge of the bank and landed beside them. The men, startled, grabbed for their guns, and then recognized their new foreman.

"Is anybody in charge here?" Pasco said shortly.

The riders looked at each other blankly, and at last one of them, a saddle-lean man with a hard angular face and curiously pale eyes, said, "I reckon not. Silas just sent us up here to hold the Forks until you came. It couldn't be done."

"Why not?"

The man shrugged. "There's no cover to speak of on this side of the Forks. When Hilderbrand's boys moved in with Otto's men and opened up on us—" He shrugged again.

Pasco recognized the rider as one of the men who had wanted to retreat the night before. But he said nothing. He moved on down the gully until he came across two Crazy Creek men firing listlessly toward the Forks from behind a washed-up cottonwood log. The men looked at him and said nothing. Pasco moved on down the creek bed for a short distance, looking for a better place to make a stand if an all-out attack really came.

There was no better place. Hornsby's riders, being experienced fighters, had figured that out for themselves. It was possible that they could take the Forks back, but it didn't seem smart to try it until they found out how many men Otto had waiting for them. Anyway, the way things stood, the Forks was a no-man's-land, and they didn't have to worry about anybody throwing up a dam as long as both sides could lay fire on the position.

Pasco made his way back to the group of riders he had first seen. "You," he pointed to the pale-eyed man, "and you," he pointed to another. "Go up ahead and join the two men on the other side of the creek. Don't waste ammunition, but be sure none of Keller's men get dug in at the Forks."

The two men picked up their carbines and began making their way through the brush along the creek bed. The others seemed to be waiting for Pasco to tell them what to do.

"Did you bring grub sacks with you when Silas sent you out?" Pasco asked.

One of the men shook his head. "Silas said he would send a chuckwagon up, but we haven't seen it."

"Get your horse from the wrangler," Pasco said. "Ride back to headquarters and remind Hornsby that men have to eat. We want grub here before nightfall. Tell him I said it."

Until then, the riders hadn't cared one way or the other about Pasco. But now they grinned, and Pasco, for the first time, felt as though he actually was the foreman. As the grub rider hurried up the creek in a stiff-legged run, Pasco said, "Maybe the rest of us had better start throwing up breastworks, in case Otto's men get a notion to run us out of here."

Shortly before sundown the chuckwagon arrived from headquarters and set up business along the creek bank at the far end of the wash. Pasco saw that the men were fed and arranged two-hour shifts of night watch, so that all of them could get some rest. After that, there was nothing to do but wait.

As the night came down, the firing stopped almost completely. It was senseless wasting cartridges by shooting into the darkness and giving their positions away. Besides, there was little chance for anyone to move up to the Forks without being heard.

Pasco bedded down with the others along the upper reaches of the stream, but sleep was difficult to come by. He lay for a long while listening to the uneasy silence of the night, wondering absently what Hornsby's next move would be. If he meant to dam off Otto's fork of the creek, it would mean taking the Forks again; and that wouldn't be easy, especially if Otto had brought up Hilderbrand's men as reinforcements.

In his mind he tried to formulate a plan of action in the event Hornsby should give the word to attack. But his interest in the fight seemed to have left him. A new kind of anger, born of frustration, began to go through him. But he knew he had to play along with Hornsby, if he was to get his chance at Otto.

He tried not to think of Myra, but there was no keeping her back now. It's no good, he told himself. She's Otto's wife now, and there's no changing it. But it wasn't true. A single bullet, well placed, could change everything.

The thought ended abruptly as a nervous burst of firing began downstream. Pasco, already tense, was on his feet immediately. He could see the vague shadows of other riders throwing blankets back, grabbing for their saddleguns. Then the firing stopped as suddenly as it had begun and Pasco called, "Stay where you are until I see what it's about."

Buckling on his .45, he ran toward the lower end of the stream. Up ahead he could see the blurred figures of two Crazy Creek riders, crouching low behind their hastily built fortification of cottonwood branches. Pasco went down to one knee beside them, his .45 in his hand.

"Who started that firing?"

One of the riders grunted. "I did. Thought I saw something moving over on the far bank."

"Are you sure you saw it?"

The rider wiped the back of his hand across his eyes. "In this darkness you can't be sure of anything."

Pasco remained motionless for a moment, thinking. Had Otto decided to try to take over the Forks at night? He doubted it. Had he sent a scout to find out how many men Hornsby had on the job? That was more likely. Pasco holstered his .45, then said, "I'm going down the creek a way and see what I can find. Hold your fire until I get back."

As quietly as possible, he slipped over the bank and eased himself into the bed of the creek. Keeping to deep shadows, he hugged the clay wall until he reached a bend, then quickly splashed into the hip-deep water and waded across the stream. Reaching the other side, he waited motionless, listening. He heard nothing.

Pasco decided that his own riders had been shooting at shadows. He lifted himself to his knees, glancing over his shoulder at the pale moon beginning to rise in the east. Suddenly the night exploded with the roar of carbine.

Something struck Pasco's ribs with the smash of a bludgeon. The impact slammed him back to the ground, and at the same instant the carbine crashed again, no more than thirty yards away. Pasco lay stunned; the breath had been driven from his lungs, and he lay gasping.

He was aware of somebody racing headlong

toward the lower end of the creek. Somehow he managed to get his .45 out of the holster and fire blindly . . . once . . . twice, in the direction of the noise. He was on his hands and knees now, shaking his head to clear it. Feeling the burning sensation high on his right side, he managed to lurch to his feet, firing once more.

Now he could hear his own riders moving clumsily forward in the darkness. Pasco yelled: "Get down the creek bank and cut him off, if you can!"

Some of the men were splashing across the creek, hurrying toward him. Others were crashing through the brush, headed toward the Forks. Otto's men below the Forks were beginning to burn bullets at them.

From down the creek Pasco heard one of his men yell, then a shattering burst of firing as two or three riders opened up with their revolvers.

A Crazy Creek rider that Pasco remembered only as Morgan climbed out of the creek bed and came toward him. "You all right, Pasco?"

"I think so. What's going on down the creek?"

Morgan, a soft-spoken, quick-eyed kid of about twenty-two, laughed shortly. "It sounded like they caught the backshooter. I reckon we'll find out pretty soon; it sounds like they're coming back."

He noticed then that Pasco was holding his

folded neckerchief against his right side. "How bad is it?" he asked.

"Just a crease. I'll look at it when we get back." Pasco and Morgan and two more riders crossed the creek again and saw three of their own men coming toward them, another man in front of them, his hands in the air. Pasco forgot the burning along his side, as he strained his eyes in the darkness, trying to see who the gunman was.

It wasn't Otto. Pasco grunted in surprise when he saw the hard, angular face of Marshal Bunt Wallace. The marshal grinned thinly, but his eyes glinted in anger as Pasco came toward him. He jerked his head at the Crazy Creek man who had brought him up. "You're the ramrod," he said to Pasco. "Tell your men to stop acting like fools and put their guns away."

"Maybe we're not such fools as you think," Pasco said grimly. "This is the second time somebody has tried to bushwhack me. If it was you, Wallace, you'll be treated like anybody else. I told you once before that you're out of your territory."

The marshal stood rigid, and for a moment he seemed too angry to speak. Suddenly he spat disgustedly. "If I had reason to kill you," he said hoarsely, "I'd shoot you in the gut, Pasco, where you could see me."

"Maybe. But I want to know why you happened

to be on the scene both times when somebody tried to kill me."

The marshal looked as if he were going to choke. He turned suddenly, ignoring the other Crazy Creek riders and their guns. "You can go to hell, Pasco. I'll tell you what I please, and when I get damned good and ready."

For a moment they ignored the sporadic fire from Otto's positions below the Forks. Stiff with anger, the marshal began making his way up the creek. One of the riders started to lunge at him, but Pasco stopped him. "It looks like we won't get any more sleep tonight," he said. "Get back to your positions and I'll take care of the marshal."

Then he quickened his step and fell in beside Wallace, walking in silence a hundred yards upstream. "This is far enough," Pasco said, when they reached the place where the crew had bedded down.

The marshal glanced at him briefly, angrily, and then began to walk on.

Pasco's .45 seemed to jump into his hand. He grabbed the marshal's shirt and jerked him around, ramming the muzzle of his revolver into Wallace's belly. "Listen to me," Pasco said, his voice tight. "I told you somebody tried twice to bushwhack me. This time I got burned across the ribs, and I'm lucky to be alive. I don't intend for it to happen again."

The marshal laughed without humor. "Then

you'd better take my advice and get out of Messina County." Pasco's hand snapped forward, crashing the barrel of his revolver against the marshal's head.

Wallace staggered back for a single step and then stood his ground.

Pasco said, "That's payment for the pistol-whipping you gave me yesterday. But that won't be the end of it if you don't start talking."

A thin trickle of blood began crawling down the marshal's cheek, toward the corner of his jaw. Methodically, he began rolling a thin cigarette, glancing at Pasco from the corner of his eye. "I rode over to Otto's place this afternoon," he said finally, "to see if I could find the horse that made the shoe marks back at Messina." He paused deliberately, striking a match on his thumbnail. "I found it," he went on flatly. "A big chestnut that belongs to one of Otto's riders. But the rider wasn't in Messina at all last night; he was guarding Otto's herd on the north range, on another horse, and there are several men to back him up on the story."

Pasco said nothing, waiting for the marshal to go on. "That's one important thing," Wallace said finally. "Another is that nobody seems to know exactly where Otto was at that time. He wasn't at the dam. He said he was going after his line riders down on the Muleshoe, but there's no way he can prove it. The riders had already got word

of the fight and had headed north by that time."
Gingerly, he touched the bruised cut on his left
cheek.

Pasco said, "That still doesn't explain about
tonight."

The marshal sighed. Most of his anger seemed
to have turned to disgust. "I got Otto's permission
to check the horses he had staked out below the
Forks. I didn't get there until a little while ago,
so I decided to stay over until morning and do
my snooping then. I saw a Rocker-O man trying
to sneak out of camp, heading up the creek with a
carbine. It looked funny to me, because Otto had
given orders for everybody to stay where they
were. I followed him."

"Did you see who he was?" Pasco's words
came softly.

"It was dark, but what little I saw looked
familiar."

"Who do you think it was?"

The marshal grinned that humorless grin again,
still fingering the cut along his cheek. "I couldn't
swear to it in court—but it looks like you were
right all along. He looked like Otto to me."

They spent the night uneasily, facing each
other on the moonlit bank of the creek. Pasco
felt that he had made an enemy unnecessarily by
accusing the marshal of the bushwhacking. To
start with, Wallace had been armed only with a
.45 when the Crazy Creek men found him, and

143

the bushwhacking had been done with a saddle-gun. Anyway, even if Wallace had been the back-shooting kind, what reason did he have for killing Pasco?

It didn't seem important, though, when he turned his mind to Otto. He had never thought of Otto as being yellow, but he could have been mistaken. Killing was one thing, but murder, lurking in darkness, was something else again.

Toward morning the soreness in Pasco's side seemed to reach from his shoulder to his knee. He stood up and walked in painful little circles to prevent the stiffness from spreading. His head felt light. He must have lost more blood that he had thought.

He found himself thinking: I hope Peg's still back at headquarters. I'll ride back in the morning when I get a chance, and have her to fix me up.

When he found his thoughts turning to Myra again, he sat down and forced himself to talk to Wallace.

"Does Otto have Hilderbrand's men helping him now?"

The marshal glanced at him, and then away. "It's your war, Pasco, not mine. I don't aim to get mixed up in it."

At last the sky in the east began to turn grey, and soon the long prairie horizon, reaching out toward Indian Territory, became edged in blood as a cold sun rose out of the darkness. Again Pasco

144

began to think of headquarters, and warm food, and soothing salve and bandages on his side.

The firing had died down long before, and now a heavy silence lay over the creek. Pasco began to realize that his wound, slight though it was, had sapped his strength. A great lethargy seemed to weight him down; the fight seemed unimportant, and his new enemy Bunt Wallace seemed unimportant. Even his burning hate for Otto Keller was becoming muddled and uncertain.

He walked down to where the horses were tethered in the damp grass along the creek bank, making mental notes of things the crew would need to see them through another day. The young rider, Morgan, came up as the wrangler cut out a horse for Pasco.

"Do you want me to keep an eye on the marshal?" the kid asked.

Morgan looked as though he needed rest as badly as Pasco did. "No," Pasco said. "Give him a horse and have one of the boys escort him off Crazy Creek range. Where he goes from there, I don't care."

Morgan shrugged. "The men want to know about supplies," he said.

"I'm going back to headquarters. You can come along and bring the stuff back."

Riding toward the Crazy Creek headquarters Pasco and Morgan crossed trails with Doc Fuller, who was returning from a visit to Otto's place. The old man was almost asleep, slouched on the seat of his buggy, his lines held lax in gnarled old hands. He glanced up as Pasco and Morgan rode alongside him. "Ah . . ." he said flatly, rubbing the stubble of grey beard on his face, "it's you, Pasco. I hope you haven't got any more men hurt. I doubt if I could stay awake long enough to take care of them."

Pasco said carefully, "You were pretty busy over at the Rocker-O, I take it."

But the doctor was not to be tricked into taking sides. He merely looked at Pasco and sighed heavily as he saw the crusted blood on Pasco's shirt and pants. "You got it too, I see. Is it bad?"

"Nothing Peg can't take care of. I was lucky."

The old man nodded dumbly, then flicked his horse listlessly with his buggy whip, and the hack lurched forward. "I'll see you at Hornsby's place."

"You want us to trail you in? Otto might have some of his men out here."

The doctor shook his head. "Otto won't bother me—not as long as I tend to my business and keep my mouth shut."

Pasco looked at Morgan and the young gunman shrugged. They moved on toward the Crazy Creek home range.

The usual activity of a working ranch was missing at the Crazy Creek as Pasco and Morgan turned their horses into the corral beside the barn. No one was to be seen except the wrangler, too old and crippled with rheumatism to be useful as a rider, and the chuck burner over at the cook shack who was halfheartedly outfitting a springless buckboard as an emergency chuckwagon.

Pasco sent Morgan to the cook shack to pick up what supplies they needed, then walked around to the front of the headquarters building to see if he could find Hornsby. He now walked with a noticeable limp.

The rancher must have seen him ride in, for he was waiting on the front porch as Pasco rounded the corner of the house. Hornsby frowned. "I didn't expect to see you back so soon. I was just getting supplies ready to send up to the Forks." Then he saw the dried blood on Pasco's clothing. "You're hurt?"

"Just burned. That's one reason I came back, but mostly I wanted to have a talk with you. Where can we be alone for a few minutes?"

The rancher rubbed his chin. "The ranch is about deserted. I pulled my line riders in this morning and sent them up to the Forks with the others. Maybe you ran across them."

Pasco shook his head, and the rancher motioned for him to follow him inside the ranch house. As they walked down a short hall, and into Hornsby's office, Pasco saw that there was nothing fancy about the Crazy Creek headquarters. It was a man's place, bare, sparsely furnished, mostly with ranch-made furniture. The building itself was constructed of pulpwood logs, the large cracks in the walls filled with a dun-colored mixture of clay and grass. There were no pictures on the walls, no carpets on the floors.

Hornsby's office was as bare as the rest of the house, containing only a rolltop desk and two straight chairs with rawhide bottoms. Hornsby nodded to Pasco to sit down, then he took the other chair himself, brushing aside the pile of ledgers and ranch books that cluttered the desk. He took a dry cigar from his vest pocket and as he rolled it in his mouth, he said, "To tell the truth, I wanted to talk to you, Pasco. But I'll hear your story first."

Pasco sat down, favoring his right side. All through the long night a vague notion had been nagging at the back of his mind; if he could only put his idea into words maybe it would relieve some of the heaviness from his shoulders, drain some of the weariness from his soul.

"Well?" Hornsby said.

"I was just thinking. We were lucky when we managed to blow up that dam of Otto's. We caught him off balance and now we've got a foothold on the Forks. But where do we go from here?"

"That's easy," Hornsby said. "While he's still off balance you'll move our men down and take control of the Forks completely, and then we'll see how Otto likes having his water dammed off from him."

Pasco smiled faintly. "It won't be that easy. He's got Hilderbrand in the fight now." He could almost feel his mind grinding to a slow halt, like some worn-out machine. Too much blood lost, he thought. Not enough sleep.

Hornsby said impatiently, "If you've got something on your mind, Pasco, come out with it."

Then Pasco said, "Maybe you'd better get somebody else for the foreman's job."

The rancher came out of his chair as though a gun had been exploded in the room. "Are you crazy!"

Pasco half smiled. "The thing has been wrong from the beginning," he said. "I hate Otto as much as you do, probably more. When I get the chance I'll kill him in a minute, but it'll be for my own reasons. It seems that I've got mixed up in a lot of things that have nothing to do with the way I hate Otto, or why I hate him, or anything else."

"You're crazy! You can't go after Otto alone, and you know it!"

"Maybe. Just the same, I keep thinking of Carl Levi. Maybe I wasn't responsible for getting him killed, but I was there in the fight, where I had no business being. And I've just started thinking of the men who were killed or hurt in that explosion at the dam." Pasco rubbed his face with his hand. "I had nothing against those men. I don't even know who they were."

"They were Otto's men," the rancher said hotly. "That ought to be enough."

But Pasco shook his head. "They were hired gunmen, just like I am, just like the rest of your riders." Then he looked up at Hornsby and almost laughed. "I had no idea what I was going to say when we came in here. It's funny how things like this can lie in the back of a man's mind and he won't even know they're there."

The rancher was making a great effort to control his anger. "Listen to me, Pasco," he said roughly. "You've been hurt. Maybe you've been a little out of your head and don't know what you're saying."

Pasco smiled. It was quite possible that Hornsby was right. He said, "Is Peg still here? Maybe if she'd just take a look at this side of mine—"

"I'll get her," Hornsby said quickly. "Why don't you come into the front room and lie down for a while. After you get some rest all this will look different to you."

Pasco said, "You know, Hornsby—" His head felt light. Loss of sleep and loss of blood were beginning to tell. "You know, Hornsby, I hate your guts."

He was vaguely aware that Hornsby left the

room and ran through the house, shouting Peg Manning's name. For what seemed a long while, Pasco sat very erect in the chair. At last he lifted himself unsteadily and made his way to the hallway and into the front room.

He got as far as the front door and knew instinctively that he would never make it outside. Besides, he had forgotten what it was that he wanted to do. His stomach fluttered. His head pounded. That's funny, he thought—it's my side that's hurt.

He walked heavily back into the room and sat down on a horsehide-covered couch. That was the last he remembered for a long while.

Chapter Eleven

When Pasco heard the heavy tramp of Hornsby's boots on the front porch, he began to pull himself out of the stupor. The front door opened and the rancher and Peg Manning came into the room.

Hornsby looked worried. "You all right, Pasco?"

"I'm fine." But he didn't feel fine.

Peg Manning said firmly, "Lie down and let me attend to the wound. Silas, have the cook get me some hot water and some bandages." The rancher went out of the room again, and Pasco felt too frayed out to resist. He lay down.

Peg said nothing until Hornsby came back with the hot water and bandages. "That will be all," she said flatly. "I can take care of it now." The rancher stood uncertainly, realizing that he was being invited to get out of his own house. After a moment he grunted, frowning, and left. Peg worked quickly, with sure hands, and when she was finished she stood up. "A few days of rest and you'll be all right. You lost more blood than you thought."

"There's not much rest to be had, with a war going on."

Something had happened to her face. She suddenly looked older. "Well," she said, in that same flat voice, "I suppose it was too much to hope for."

Pasco, not understanding, grinned faintly. "It's just a scratch. No need to worry about it."

Suddenly she was angry. It showed in her eyes, in the line of her mouth. "Do you think I'm worried about you?" she asked tightly. "Do you think I'd allow myself to worry over a hired gunman? A few minutes ago I had hopes for you—but not anymore." She laughed suddenly, harshly. "You even had Silas worried for a few minutes. He thought you were going to quit him. He was afraid you had decided there were better things to live for than killing and revenge."

The unexpected outburst left Pasco stunned for a moment. At last he stood up, somehow managing to keep his voice calm. "This is men's business, Peg. I guess women can't be expected to understand it."

"There are plenty of men," she said harshly, "who manage to live without killing."

There was nothing he could say to that. He walked across the room, his side still stiff and sore, and stood looking out at Hornsby's sun-baked front yard. He heard Peg coming toward him, felt her standing beside him.

She said, "Then you didn't mean any of the things you said to Hornsby?"

"I must have been a little out of my head." He turned, looking at her. "Last night Otto tried to kill me," he said. "He'll try again, and keep on trying, until he finally succeeds. It's him or me, Peg."

But it wasn't much of an argument. If he really wanted to change, he could get out of this particular part of Texas. There were a lot of ways a man could avoid a killing if he wanted to. But why should he care what a dressmaker thinks of him?

The answer came slowly, and he found it hard to believe. Myra had ceased to haunt him. When he looked at Peg, Myra ceased to be a part of him. He was free. Methodically now, Pasco turned the thing over in his mind, asking himself questions whose answers he already knew.

Peg Manning could see the change taking place inside him. She stood silently for a long moment, and then she said, "What is it, John?"

"I'm not sure." And then he acted on pure impulse. He put out his arms and was somehow holding Peg against him. She didn't fight. Her eyes were wide as he held her, almost roughly, but she made no sound. Suddenly he forced her head back and kissed her. Finally, when he let her go, he said hoarsely, "I guess I'm sure now."

She seemed very calm, as though nothing unusual had happened. "You're sure of what, John?"

"Myra has lost her magic. I had the feeling that it had happened, but I couldn't be sure until I kissed you. There was just you, Peg. No ghosts, no childhood dreams rose up to spoil it." He felt suddenly strong, as though he had been released from chains. "Thanks, Peg. Thanks for helping me."

She looked at him blankly. Only a man in the grip of his own ego could have missed the meaning behind that look. It took John Pasco several seconds to see it and to understand that Peg Manning was in love with him. She had mistaken his selfish experiment for something else, and the knowledge made Pasco uncomfortable and ashamed. I'm not the man for you, Peg, he wanted to say. I'm like a runaway wagon nearing the bottom of a steep grade. There's no future with me. You deserve a better man, and you'll find him, some day.

But the words were only in his mind, and he couldn't make a sound as she stood there waiting for some kind of explanation. Outside, he heard the sound of a running horse. The beat of hoofs came nearer, and the sound mingled with the muffled thud of boots running across the ranch yard. "I'm sorry, Peg," Pasco said at last. "I shouldn't have done that, I guess." Then, not looking at her, he turned to the front door to see what the confusion was about.

The lone rider was turning his lathered horse into the far corral as Pasco stepped onto the front porch. He could see Hornsby, fat and puffing, talking heatedly to the rider. Pasco jumped off the porch and a dagger of pain slashed his side. I hope it's not serious trouble, he thought as he began running. I don't know how long I can last if the trouble's bad.

Hornsby was yelling to the wrangler as Pasco reached the corral. Then the rancher turned on Pasco. "Hell's broke loose at the Forks! Round up every man that can ride and get up there in a hurry!"

"What's the trouble?" Pasco spoke to the rider, who seemed much calmer than Hornsby.

"Trouble aplenty," the rider said wearily. "Old Hilderbrand brought his men around behind us last night some time. About an hour ago they hit us, and ran off most of our horses. Otto held his own men down below the Forks, so they've got us boxed in. They'll have us cleaned out before long, I reckon, if we don't get some help."

Pasco's first impulse was to curse. He felt hot anger at the men for letting a thing like this happen—anger at himself for leaving. With an effort he put the anger down and forced himself to think coolly. One thing was clear; Otto was desperate, or he and Hilderbrand would never have split their forces. He was depending on suddenness of attack to rout Hornsby, gambling that sheer surprise would outweigh the Crazy Creek's edge in numbers.

And, Pasco thought now, if I don't think of

something, Otto's strategy will succeed. He turned on his heel and saw Morgan coming from one of the far barns with a loaded supply wagon. "Leave the wagon!" he shouted to the young gunman. "Cut out a fresh horse; I've got a job for you!"

Morgan pulled up, and then dropped down from the wagon seat and started in a lazy lope toward the corral.

Pasco turned to Hornsby. "How many men have we got riding line?"

The rancher wiped his sweating face. "Just two. Everybody else was sent up to the Forks."

"Two men." Not much of an army to stage a diverting action with, but they would have to do. One thing was in Pasco's favor—he could depend on Otto and Hilderbrand having all their riders already in the action. Pasco turned and started running toward the corral where Morgan had just cut out a prancing bay gelding. It took only a moment to sketch the situation and give the gunman his instructions.

Morgan shrugged and grinned. "It looks like it's going to be a big day, all right."

Pasco leaned against the corral, feeling his side grow damp. The bandages were already pulling loose, but there was no time to think about that. Otto was making a final, desperate play for success—that was the important thing. And he had to be stopped. Pasco tightened his belt to help hold the bandages in place, and called to the old wrangler for fresh horses.

Hornsby yelled hoarsely, "Dammit, Pasco, why don't you get to the Forks!"

Anger began to rise, but again Pasco put it down. "Are you aiming to join the battle with us, Silas?" he asked dryly.

The rancher flushed. "You know I can't go off and leave the ranch to take care of itself. It's your job to take care of Otto and Hilderbrand. That's why I hired you."

"Then I'll do it my own way." The rancher's cowardice made Pasco cringe inside. He stood for a moment, watching Morgan fork the big gelding out of the ranch yard and head to the south, then he turned to the other rider and said, "Get yourself a new horse, cowboy. We're about to do some riding."

Peg Manning was out in the back yard as the two men circled the barn and saddle shed and headed toward the Forks. Pasco saw her, and for a moment he thought of riding over to her and saying something to reassure her. But he only lifted his hand in a small gesture and touched his horse with blunted spurs.

The two men rode steadily, silently, as the monotonous flatland passed treadmill-like beneath their horses' hoofs. Pasco rode without regard for the pain in his side. This would be the day for settling with Otto—that was the thing he thought of, it was the only important thing. Only after they had raised the Forks, as they plunged down the last gentle slope toward the wooded stream, did Pasco remember Myra and the date with her that he had not even remembered. He felt like laughing. It was good to be free and unhaunted.

Now they could hear the muted spat of rifle fire from the creek, and the rider beside Pasco began riding lower in his saddle. "You'll have to lead the way!" Pasco called.

The rider nodded, riding hard now, as the insignificant gunfire bursts grew louder and more deadly. He motioned toward a stand of cottonwood, where a good portion of the firing seemed to be coming from. "That's where the boys were when I left them! I hope they're still there!"

If they aren't, Pasco thought, we won't live long enough to worry about it. Then he heard the rush and whine of a bullet burning the air over his head. He ducked instinctively, unable to judge where the assault was coming from. If Otto's men had taken over that clump of cottonwood— Well, there was no use worrying about it now. They covered the last hundred yards at a hard run, driving their horses through the tangle of brush along the creek bank. Pasco and the rider dumped out of their saddles, stumbling toward the protection of the creek. A figure rose from behind a rotting pulpwood stump, and yelled: "We're over here, Pasco!"

The place was suddenly alive with bullets smashing through the thicket. The rider dived headlong for the creek and Pasco fell on his face behind the stump. He lay there for a moment, getting his breath, trying not to think of the crawling dampness along his hip. At last he looked up at the long-faced, unruffled man crouching beside him, recognizing him as one of Hornsby's gunmen, a man named Mayhew. "Where are the others?" Pasco asked.

"Down in the creek and over on the other bank. Wherever they can find something to get behind—which ain't the easiest thing to do. We've got Otto below us and old Hilderbrand behind us." Lying on his stomach, gazing idly over the sights of his carbine, Mayhew seemed completely calm. The firing, Pasco noticed, had slackened off somewhat. "I hope," the Crazy Creek gunman drawled, "that Hornsby's sending us some help up here."

"We'll get help after a while, but we'll have to hold on for an hour or so ourselves. How bad has it been?"

"It ain't been good. They run off our horses, and now they've got us nailed down here, like shooting fish in a barrel." He spat a stream of tobacco juice over the barrel of his carbine, then listened for a moment to the sound of groaning coming from the creek bed below. "That's Barstow," he said.

Pasco remembered Barstow as a tough kid about Morgan's age; one of Hornsby's first to hire on at fighting pay. He didn't sound tough now. He sounded like any other man with a bullet inside him.

Pasco lay still for a moment, listening, wondering when Otto and Hilderbrand would make their big play. He turned to Mayhew and said, "Help me get the men out of that creek bed. It will be a death trap when Otto and Hilderbrand start bringing their forces together."

Mayhew shrugged. They began crawling toward the creek bank, worming their way through briar thickets and weeds. Now and then a rifle would explode, the sound bellowing and mushrooming between the clay walls of the stream, but the concentrated effort of attack was absent now. More than likely, Pasco thought, the two ranchers were gathering their strength. The attack would come soon enough. Still on their bellies, the two men slipped over the edge of the creek bank, half falling down to the water's edge in a small landslide of crumbling clay. Immediately half a dozen rifles exploded from up above, but the bullets smacked harmlessly into the red earth banks. There were eight men down there, jammed into the tight bend. Safe enough as long as Otto and Hilderbrand stayed in the creek bed themselves. But when they decided to make an assault from above—Pasco didn't like to think about that.

Mayhew was down on one knee, talking to Barstow. Pasco moved over to them and said, "Is he hit bad?"

"I don't think so. The bullet went in here below the hip and came out down here." Somebody had cut away part of the kid's trousers and bandaged the wounds tightly in both places. "We're moving out of the creek bed," Mayhew said. "Two of you men come and give me a hand with Barstow."

Until now the Crazy Creek men had said nothing. They leaned or crouched against the walls of the creek secure in their knowledge that rifles could not shoot around corners. As long as they stayed huddled together in that tight bend, they reasoned, there was nothing to worry about. Now one of the men turned quietly away from his position along the water's edge. "I reckon," he said flatly, "we'll just stay down here in the creek bed. Barstow got his up there on the bank. If he'd stayed down here with the rest of us, it never would of happened."

It was the pale-eyed rider, the one that Pasco had had trouble with at the dam. Now the other men were looking at Mayhew, and one of them said, "Carson's right. The healthiest place on this creek is right here in the bend."

"What if Keller and Hilderbrand try to attack

from above?" Pasco asked, looking at Carson.

Carson laughed shortly. "I guess their boys are no more anxious to get out in the open than we are."

"Just the same, we're getting out of this creek bed." I should have fired that man, Pasco thought angrily. I should have set him packing after that affair at the dam. An uneasy stillness fell over the creek as the men hesitated at Pasco's order. Their eyes turned first to Carson, then to the foreman, as though there were some doubt in their minds as to who was boss. Pasco could feel his grip of authority being broken.

"Get up on the bank," he said again to the men, his eyes still on Carson. Reluctantly, one of the men took a step forward, and then stopped abruptly as Carson said, "Go on and get yourself killed, if you want to. Me, I'm staying down here. How about the rest of you boys?"

The moment of indecision was over. The man stepped back to his position against the clay wall, and the other riders held their places. Carson grinned thinly. Wearily, Pasco understood that he had lost his hold completely, and he wondered for one dull moment if getting it back was worth the trouble.

But the moment of defeat was brief, and Pasco's anger came back with a rush. Otto was less than a hundred yards away, fighting for his life, and Pasco wasn't going to be stopped now—

163

not by a gutless killer like Carson. Watching the man carefully, Pasco said softly, "It looks like you've forgotten who's giving orders to this crew, Carson."

The man tensed, but held his grin. He was no longer afraid of Pasco's strength—he could see the weary glassiness in the foreman's eyes. He said, "I'm not taking orders that I can't see any sense in. And the rest of the boys ain't either."

The line was drawn, the time for talk had passed. Before the words were out of Carson's mouth, Pasco stepped forward and hit him full in the face. The suddenness of the attack stunned Carson for a moment. He reeled back, dropping his carbine. As he hit the creek bank he grabbed for his holstered .45, but Pasco was already on top of him. Grasping the man's hand, Pasco twisted hard, up and back. In one savage effort, he beat the hand against the hard clay and broke the man's grip on the revolver.

Already, Pasco was gasping for air. His arms became heavy as he wrestled silently with Carson, and he knew he would have to end it quickly or not at all. Carson recovered quickly from the shock of the first assault. A great rage took hold of him as he felt his revolver falling from his hand. With sudden savageness, he kicked out with the sharp toe of his boot, and explosive nausea rushed into Pasco's throat as he took the kick in his groin. He went down to his knees, then thrust himself backward as Carson shot the boot in again. In a desperate effort to gain time, Pasco reached out blindly, caught the boot in his arms and pulled the man down with him. They rolled down the brief slope and into the cold water.

The Crazy Creek riders made no sound at all as they watched the battle rage savagely along the creek bank and finally into the stream itself. No words of encouragement were uttered for either man as Pasco and Carson, locked together, rolled into the stream and the muddy water splashed over them.

Carson grunted as the water rolled over them, and that was the first sound that either man had made. They splashed for a moment, uncertainly, clumsily, attempting to gain footing in the slippery mud. Waist deep in water, they came toward each other again. Carson lashed out and Pasco began to fall as a fist crashed into his ribs. It was like falling in a nightmare, without beginning and without end. Pasco reached out blindly and tried to pull Carson down with him. His hands, slippery with mud, slid off Carson's arm, and Pasco floundered to his knees. Carson came on with a rush and the two men closed again. Pasco, unable to find footing in the mud, felt the last of his strength dissolving in the sluggish water. Savage now, with victory in sight,

Carson hurled himself at Pasco, snapping an arm around the foreman's neck.

Pasco clawed helplessly at the tightening hold on his throat. He felt his breath cut off, he felt Carson forcing him back, back, and finally the cold water was flowing over his face.

The fight went out of him. He was suddenly tired to death of fighting, tired of running, and he could almost welcome a quiet, flowing end to all of it. His head pounded. There was a searing flame in his chest and he fumbled blindly in the watery ooze of the creek bottom. His hand touched something, and he tugged weakly as the life was being choked out of him. He jerked, realizing that he had hold of Carson's boot. He twisted it, and suddenly the boot began to give, began to slip in the mud. Pasco felt under water for Carson's leg. He shoved one fist behind the knee and then pushed violently, and Carson came crashing down on top of him.

The smothering sensation of hopelessness was suddenly gone. As Carson released his hold, Pasco shot to the top of the water, gasping for breath, dragging huge gulps of cool air into his burning lungs. With new life, he grasped the back of Carson's shirt before the man could fall. He jerked the man around and drove his fist brutally into Carson's groin. That's in payment for that kick! he thought savagely. Carson's face blanched. Helplessly, he dropped his hands and

Pasco hit him again, and then again, driving him backward toward the bank.

Finally Carson was down. Pasco stood dumbly, his arms hanging, as the gunman lay half submerged in the muddy water. He stood there for a long while, dripping and slimy with mud, still gulping air into his aching lungs. Finally, he reached down and grasped the collar of Carson's shirt, dragged him heavily to the water's edge, and dropped him. With a touch of wildness in his eyes, he looked at his men. All he said was, "We're getting out of this creek bed. Somebody give Mayhew a hand with Barstow and Carson." He started heavily toward the creek bank and began climbing up the slippery wall. One by one, the men deserted their positions in the bend and came after him.

There was no firing now. The countryside lay dead and still under the blistering sun as the last of the men straggled to the top of the bank. Pasco took out his .45 and began cleaning it on the tail of his shirt. "Two men over there." He pointed to a shallow depression in the ground in the midst of a briar thicket. He placed the other men behind stumps, rocks, or whatever they could find to hide behind. Pasco and Mayhew took up their positions behind a rotting oak log on high ground overlooking the bend in the creek.

Pasco punched the wet cartridges from his revolver and replaced them with dry ones from

Mayhew's belt. "That Carson's going to cause trouble," Mayhew said idly. "Maybe you ought to of let him drown."

"Carson's in no condition to cause trouble soon." Then they both heard the rustle of brush. Mayhew glanced at Pasco. Very gently, the gunman jacked a cartridge into his short carbine.

"It looks like we're about to have callers."

Pasco raised himself to one elbow. "We're just lucky they didn't decide to come sooner." Another rustle—somewhere behind them this time—and both men tensed. Otto and Hilderbrand were trying to box them in. Pasco raised one arm, caught the attention of the two riders in the briar thicket, and pointed toward the sound. The men had already heard it, and they didn't like it.

"They don't know when they're lucky," Mayhew drawled. "They'd really have somethin' to worry about if they'd stuck down there in the creek bed."

Pasco hardly heard the gunman. He listened hard with all his senses—the way a wild animal listens. He sniffed the air, as though he could smell danger there. He used his eyes to guide his ears—and at last he saw them coming through the brush on the far side of the creek. One man, then another, and another. They came crawling on their bellies and elbows, cradling saddleguns in the crooks of their arms.

"Keller's boys," Mayhew said quietly, watching

them over the sights of his carbine. He chuckled soundlessly. "Otto's going to be mighty disappointed when he finds we're not down there in that bend."

Pasco could feel nervousness in the air. The men were beginning to understand now why he had taken them out of the trap. They were angry now, and some of them were frightened. Pasco motioned again for the men to stay down. I just hope some fool doesn't give our position away, he thought tensely. I just hope Otto or Hilderbrand will step into their own trap.

He wanted it to be Otto, but the chances were against that. The range was too great even for carbines, and Otto was bringing his men up too carefully. Hilderbrand, Pasco thought. He's the one we'll have to concentrate on. And Mayhew was thinking the same thing. The gunman was ignoring the far creek bank now, putting his attention on the clumsier snappings and rustlings that were coming from behind them. I hope Morgan is taking care of his job, Pasco thought. I hope he takes care of it in time to do us some good.

"There they come," Mayhew said calmly. "Downstream there, maybe a hundred yards." He shook his head sadly. "You'd think they could be a little quieter about it, wouldn't you?"

It was Hilderbrand's men this time. About six of them, Pasco judged, but it sounded like a small army as they came crashing through the undergrowth. Pasco felt elation spiral up inside him—this was what he had been waiting for, a chance to cut Otto's forces in half. Knowing that the men were watching him, he raised his hand the slightest bit.

"Now?" Mayhew asked, still squinting over the sights of his carbine.

Pasco drew his revolver and nodded. "Now."

Chapter Twelve

Hilderbrand's crew didn't have a chance. The briar thicket exploded with the sound of carbines and revolvers, springing Otto's trap on his own men. It lasted only a moment, and it would have been funny if it hadn't been so deadly. Hilderbrand's men broke and scattered, some of them diving headlong down the steep embankment and into the creek, others running blindly into trees, tripping, falling in their panic, then getting up and running again.

Pasco saw one man go down as though a sledge had struck him from behind. He got up almost immediately, holding a red arm with one hand, and disappeared around the bend of the creek. Mayhew laughed quietly as he emptied his carbine and took to his revolver. "I guess this is the last of old Hilderbrand for a while!"

Pasco caught a glimpse of the old rancher trying to throw himself into the path of his retreating men, yelling at them, cursing them. Pasco came up to one knee, knowing that they could not let up now. For just a moment he had the rancher in his sights. All I have to do, he thought, is squeeze the trigger. Don't give Hilderbrand a chance to gather his forces and box you in again!

But he couldn't do it. Killing in cold blood

was not in him, and at last the revolver began to waver and he let his arm drop to his side. From the other side of the creek Otto and his men had opened fire, giving Hilderbrand's men a chance to make their escape.

"This spot's getting unhealthy," Mayhew said, as a carbine bullet came crashing into their rotten log. "Hadn't we better move down the creek a piece?"

"We've got to see that Hilderbrand's crew stays scattered for a while." Pasco stood up and zigzagged across the clearing, yelling for the men to follow him. This was the kind of fighting hired gunmen liked, shooting at men's backs. They crashed through the underbrush, down one creek bank and up the other, stopping now and then to pump lead in the direction of Hilderbrand's fleeing crew.

"That's enough," Pasco called at last. "It'll take Hilderbrand all day to get them together again. If he ever does." The men paused, some of them stretching out on the creek bank after the run. "By hell," Mayhew said, "a man needs a horse for this kind of thing." Panting, the gunman began reloading his .45. "Now that he's seen his trap didn't work, you reckon Keller'll give up?"

"Not if I know Keller."

"What do you aim to do?"

"There's just one thing to do. He'll be coming after us in a minute—we'll just have to find a place here on the creek and stand him off until something happens."

It didn't take Otto long to get his counterattack started. For a moment Pasco was tempted to meet him headlong, to have the thing finished once and for all—but a touch of caution held him back. The prospect of more bloodshed stopped him. It was Keller he was after, and Keller alone.

When they began to hear the sound of movement upstream, Mayhew glanced sidewise at Pasco, jacking a cartridge into the chamber of his carbine. "Sounds like Keller means business this time. Reckon he figures it'll take more'n tricks to rout us out."

"Spread out along the creek bank," Pasco said, without looking back at the men. There was no argument this time, and no questions. The gunmen spread out along the upper bank, even Carson did as he was told. A single rifle shot started the siege. From upstream the sound puffed up and the heavy slug came ripping blindly through the thicket of weeds and grass.

Beside him, Mayhew fired one round from his carbine and cursed.

There was no way of knowing what Otto was thinking or what he was planning. It was a good bet, though, Pasco decided, that Keller was simply going to try to keep them pinned down and hope that Hilderbrand's men would come back and give him some help. Pasco pulled his revolver, but held his fire. I should have put a bullet in old Hilderbrand, he thought, while I had the chance. And then, for some unknown reason, a picture of Peg Manning flashed in his mind, and he was glad he had let the rancher go.

"Look," he said to Mayhew, "do you think you can ramrod this bunch for a while?"

The gunman shrugged, neither flattered nor annoyed. "You aim to take a vacation?"

"I aim to see if I can find out what Otto is up to." He holstered his revolver, then paused for a moment before crawling away. "If anything breaks I want you to move the men down to the Forks and hold it until you hear from me or Hornsby."

The gunman shrugged once more and nodded as Pasco shouldered his way into a heavy stand of brush. Within a few minutes he was out of sight of his own men, kneeling in the tall weeds directly across the creek from Otto's crew. The sudden fit of firing had played out, and there was only an occasional carbine bark. Pasco wished he could see what Otto was up to, but it was impossible through the heavy undergrowth. One thing was sure—Keller would have decided by now he couldn't expect much help from Hilderbrand, and that meant Otto would have to start planning another move.

The creek was suddenly quiet again; too quiet for Pasco's liking. Had Otto moved his men out, or was he playing possum, waiting for the Crazy Creek men to make a wrong move? There was only one way of knowing for sure, and that was to cross the creek and see if they were still there. It was a fine idea, Pasco thought wryly, if an early burial was what you wanted.

He decided to move farther upstream, on the chance that Otto was trying to come around that way and get behind them. He had crawled only a few yards when he began to hear the sucking sounds of boots in mud and water. A few yards more and Pasco could see over the embankment. He smiled. It was one of Keller's men wading the creek.

The man, holding his carbine high as he sloughed through the water, paused for a moment, looked both upstream and downstream, then continued on to the near bank. Pasco lost sight of him as he climbed the bank and disappeared into the brush. Several moments passed as silence settled over the creek again. Pasco waited tensely, expecting the rest of Otto's crew to begin wading the stream. When nothing happened, it occurred to Pasco that the man he had seen must have been the last one. Otto must have his crew already over here!

Very carefully, Pasco began backing away from the lip of the creek. He listened hard but could hear no sound. Pasco could imagine that eyes were watching him, following him from behind the sights of carbines. Why else would they remain so quiet? Why didn't they move? Why didn't they swing wide around Pasco's crew and drive them into the creek? There was no sound at all, and Pasco could almost believe that the man in the creek had only been his imagination. He began to breathe easier as he backed away—and then the creek seemed to explode with sound.

The sharp bark of a saddlegun shattered the silence, and on top of it came one bellowing explosion after another. As Pasco fell onto his belly he heard the vicious snarl of bullets ripping through the patches of weeds—and he thought: this is crazy! Otto wouldn't give his position away like this!

Behind him, Pasco heard his own men crashing through the brush to face the new attack, and he heard Mayhew yelling and cursing, driving them forward.

"What the hell's goin' on here?" The gaunt gunman dropped down beside Pasco and fired two rounds from his carbine.

"It looks like Otto's crossed the creek," Pasco shouted. "I guess he wanted to get behind us and shove us over the bank."

"This is a hell of a way to go about it!" Mayhew spat. "See that bend up there? He's got his back to the wall with no place to go. It looks like Keller just stepped into his own trap!"

Until now Pasco hadn't noticed the sharp

crook in the creek, where the firing was coming from. But he saw it now, and a vicious elation went through him. Mayhew was right—Otto had outsmarted himself this time. Pasco could spread his own men out and force the Keller crew into the bend.

He stood up now, ignoring the crack of rifles and snap of bullets. He sent Mayhew over to his right to spread his men out. "Force them into that bend! Mayhew, get the men spread out there!"

For a moment the Crazy Creek crew worked like a well-trained squad of infantry. They could sense the importance of that bend. They were old hands at killing, and they knew a death trap when they saw one. Still, in the midst of his elation, Pasco felt uneasiness begin to stir. Keller was too smart for a blunder like this. Even as he thought it, as the Crazy Creek men began their charge on the bend, the lower end of the stream seemed to explode in fury.

A shattering burst of rifle fire crashed down around them and Pasco stood frozen, unable to move. Otto had outsmarted him. Keller had deliberately sent one or two of his men across the creek as bait and had then moved the major part of his crew around to hit at Pasco's rear. Dumbly, Pasco watched his own men flee in panic. He watched them run directly into the death trap at the bend. And then, in the midst of the noise and confusion, he heard the unmistakable sound of a lead slug striking flesh. Mayhew spun half around, as though he had been jerked on a string by some giant hand. His carbine thudded into the deep grass as the gunman bent double, clutching his middle with both hands.

The gunman fell over clumsily, like a child who had not yet mastered the art of walking. He lay in the grass, his knees drawn up to his chin, not making a sound. Pasco was jarred from his moment of stupor. He dropped down beside Mayhew, knowing instinctively that the man was dying. There was nothing anyone could do. Mayhew looked up at him, his face drawn as tight as leather stretched on a saddle tree. He opened his mouth but made no sound. And then, still looking at Pasco with vacant eyes, he died. Rage took hold of Pasco as he gently closed the dead, staring eyes. This is something else that you'll pay for, Otto, he thought grimly.

But the tables had turned. They had jumped at Otto's bait, and now they were in the trap that they had set for Otto. There was only one thing to do now—fight with their backs to the wall, and when they couldn't hold out any longer . . . With sudden savagery, Pasco got to his feet, his revolver in his hand, and began retreating toward the bend. He ignored the slashing rain of lead, bellowing orders to his men, bringing a kind of hopeless order out of blind confusion. Outwardly he remained calm, but inside he was almost insane with rage. How Otto must be laughing!

Almost singlehandedly, Pasco blunted the point of Otto's attack. He didn't see Otto himself— there was no time to search him out. There was only time to fire and run, and fire again, and finally he stumbled, half fell down the sloping bank of the bend. Only then did he fully realize the hopelessness of their position. Behind them was sheer, unscalable clay; in front of them and at either end of the bend Otto's men came pouring in to cut them off.

It was then that his nostrils quivered with a new, sharp smell that punctured the heavy air like needles. Smoke! he thought. Morgan! For one wild moment Pasco felt the crazy urge to laugh. Morgan had done his job! The young gunman had somehow rounded up the line riders and they were putting fire to Otto's range below the Forks, following Pasco's orders. There was just one thing wrong—they were too late.

It had been Pasco's hope that a grass fire at the right time would drive Keller's men away from the creek. The least he had hoped for was that a prairie fire would cause a diversion and give his men a chance to get the jump on Otto. But it was too late. Otto's trap had sprung. It had been a fine plan, but it all came too late. Damn you, Morgan, he thought helplessly, why couldn't you have started that fire ten minutes ago? Five minutes ago!

Otto's charge had halted momentarily. They sniffed the smoke, trying to figure it out. Great white billowing clouds of it rose above the tall cottonwoods and hung suspended like a pale shroud. Tattered ribbons of smoke drifted up the draw, swirling and spinning like grey ghosts along the banks of the creek. Almost immediately Pasco heard a bellow of anger. Otto, hiding somewhere in the weeds, was shouting to his men to close the gap and move in on the bend to finish the job they had set out to do. Then they could take care of the grass fire.

From somewhere a horse screamed in panic. Now smoke was rolling into the draw like an endless unfolding blanket. Pasco stood helplessly as the choking cloud came down on top of them. He watched his men disappear in the whiteness. He could hear their coughing and cursing, but he could see nothing. And at last the importance of that smothering blanket of smoke came to him—Morgan was doing some good, after all! The smoke was a cover, and behind it they had a chance to escape the trap!

Almost instantly Pasco began shouting new orders to his men—but they had fled. He could hear them clawing, scrambling, running in every direction, and Pasco realized that his private army had deserted. They had left him to finish the war by himself, in the best way he could.

Tears were streaming down his face now as he

tried to cough the choking smoke from his lungs. Blindly, he climbed the bank and stood for a moment in the midst of swirling whiteness. The screaming of the horses became more insistent, and Pasco heard the thud and scamper of hoofs as they began to break away. Otto's horses. That was good. And Otto's men had deserted him too, in the confusion, for Pasco could hear them running. It was all even now, just Otto and himself coming together in the smoke.

But Otto had disappeared with the others, and after a few minutes Pasco was forced to retreat himself. He stumbled upstream, and at last he reached a place where the air was cool and clean. He went down to his hands and knees and gulped the fresh air into his lungs. All around him lay blackened, smoldering acres of burned grass. Out of a black gully a black face appeared, and then a smoke-grimed figure of a man arose and came toward him. It was Morgan.

"Pasco?" he gasped.

The only sound now was the crackle of the grass fire as it raced downstream over the sun-parched prairie. Pasco stared at the young gunman, all that was left of the army that Hornsby had turned over to him.

Morgan went down to one knee, wiping his face, staring back at the retreating curtain of smoke. "Well," he said finally, "that was one hell of a fire, I'll say that much. That grass went up like gunpowder when we put the torch to it."

"Where are the line riders you were supposed to pick up?" Pasco said abruptly.

Morgan laughed. "Where's the rest of the crew? The whole outfit dissolved in that smoke, looks like. I guess most of them have had enough of this range war to last a spell."

Pasco looked at him. "And you?"

The gunman shrugged. "I'll stay—as long as I get fighting pay. Besides, I've got nowhere else to go."

For a long while Pasco said nothing. Well, he thought, it's simple enough. This is Otto's range and he's on it somewhere. All you have to do is find him, and then it will be settled, one way or the other. He got to his feet and looked at Morgan. "Have you got a horse?"

"Staked out down in the gully."

Without bothering to explain, Pasco walked down the gully until he came to the nervous, high-strung gelding. Morgan could walk, if he had to. He wouldn't like it, but Pasco didn't worry about that. He had to have a horse, and sooner or later he and Otto would come together.

He rode out of the gully and away from the burned-out draw, not even looking back as Morgan shouted to him. He rode straight for the Keller headquarters. He had no plan now; he simply wanted to find Otto and get it over with. Ahead, he sighted a scattering of cattle about a watering hole, and he felt his parched insides quiver with the ache for a drink.

Kneeling at the muddy edge of the pool, he drank slightly upstream from his horse. When he tried to lift himself he realized how near exhaustion he was. His side was a dull swath of pain that he was almost accustomed to—but the limpness of his legs and arms was something else. Instead of returning to his horse, he sat beside a young cottonwood—and that was when the thought came to him. Why should I hunt for Otto? Sooner or later he'll come to me. The watering hole was the answer. It lay between the Forks and Otto's headquarters, and the rancher was almost sure to stop there before going home.

Pasco smiled grimly. He took out his .45 and cleaned it carefully. He wiped the cartridges clean and replaced them in the revolver, and then he took the gelding down to the lower end of the watering hole and picketed him in the deep grass. I've waited five years, he thought; I can wait a few hours more. He dozed off once and awakened with that same uneasy feeling that he was being watched. I need rest, he thought. I need a lot of things. Well, there'll be time for that later. . . .

The day dragged itself out and died. Pasco waited. Night came down and the smell of burned grass hung over the prairie, and a pale moon came out. Pasco waited.

It was morning again before Otto came. He

appeared in the distance, the blazing halo of the sun at his back. Pasco began stepping back, then realized that a wall of brush hid him from Otto's view. As Otto came on, slouched and heavy in the saddle, the weight of a sleepless night heavy upon him, a dead silence seemed to fall over the prairie. No frogs croaked at the pool's edge. The June flies seemed to have stilled their dry fluttering. Then, out of the quietness, a sound startled Pasco. He wheeled as the sound of a snapping twig hit him like a gunshot, his gun hand poised near the butt of his revolver.

There was nothing to be seen but the tangle of brush. Slowly, he began to breathe again. It was nothing. He convinced himself of that before he turned again to Otto.

Keller was less than a hundred yards away now, riding in a deep stupor, and Pasco was shocked as he saw how the rancher had changed. Otto was bigger, heavier, and a great deal older than he had been five years ago. Looking at him, Pasco could almost believe that he was looking at old Jules Keller, Otto's father. Hard, tallowlike fat bulged above the collar of his sweat-stained shirt. His cartridge belt cut into the fat of his belly like a string drawn tight around a fat sausage. His small eyes were mere slits in a puffy face, his heavy jowls hung flaccid.

Myra's husband! Pasco thought. He found himself laughing silently as Otto reined up at the edge of the pool. He watched Keller untie his neckerchief and wipe his grimy face; then the rancher got down on his knees and drank deeply beside his horse. Pasco stepped out of the brush with suddenness and Keller merely raised his face and stared with animal-like dumbness.

"It's been a long time, Otto."

Those small eyes flashed. "Well, you've got me where I can't fight back. What's holding your gun, Pasco?"

Pasco breathed deeply, hungrily, and only then did he realize that he had been holding his breath. "Get up," he said hoarsely. "When I kill you, Otto, it'll be from the front. I won't shoot from behind, like you."

Keller blinked. "If you let me get up," he said with deadly calm, "I'll kill you, Pasco."

Surprised, Pasco heard himself laugh. "You're welcome to try. But I won't have my back to you this time."

Half off his knees, Keller blinked again, puzzled. He settled back on all fours, like some fat bear ready to lunge. "That's the second time you mentioned backshooting. Now I want to know what you mean."

Pasco frowned. He could almost believe that Otto was innocent of the two bushwhacking attempts, but the evidence was too great. Hadn't Bunt Wallace traced the horse to the Rocker-O? Didn't the marshal follow behind Otto the night before, on the creek? "You haven't forgotten the wagon yard already, have you, Otto? That night that you tried to burn me down with a rifle?"

Heat rushed to Otto's face and he spat his disgust at the ground. "Somebody's been filling you full of lies and you haven't got sense enough to know it. I haven't been off my range since the first fight at the dam." There was deadly seriousness in Keller's voice. Otto gazed at Pasco coldly with those slitted eyes. "I would have killed you in a minute, Pasco. I hate your guts. But I wouldn't bushwhack you. I wouldn't give away the pleasure of watching you die!"

Pasco hardly heard the words. He only saw the hate, bright and alive, in Keller's eyes.

Chapter Thirteen

A second had passed—no more—since Otto had said it, and now the two men stared hotly at each other, Otto still on all fours, and Pasco in his half crouch, ready to draw. Then another thought struck Pasco and for a fleeting instant left him numb.

He thought, am I so much better than Otto, after all? Myra played us against each other—she's the one I should have hated. She had the power over Otto; she could have saved me from prison if she had wanted to. He had reason for hating Otto, but the passion was leaving him, the fire was dying. For the most part he had deceived himself, he had carefully channeled his hate and directed it; through five long years he had nursed it and kept it alive. Now that the time had come to collect, he felt nothing but emptiness.

With animal cunning, Otto's quick eyes followed Pasco's every move, ready at any instant to lunge, claw, fight to the death. The look of cunning became panic when Pasco, without a word, moved his hand and jerked his revolver free from its holster. Then the panic faded and Otto's face twisted with rage, thinking that Pasco had never intended to give him a chance for his life. Keller had no chance of reaching his gun.

Both hands were on the ground, half supporting the upper bulk of his body.

Keller didn't believe it when the explosion failed to come. Braced for the shock of the bullet, his mouth fell open in bewilderment when Pasco said:

"I'm not going to kill you, Otto. Unbuckle your cartridge belt and stand up."

Wearily, Pasco began stepping back, his gun still trained on Otto as the rancher began lifting himself from the ground.

"Unbuckle your cartridge belt," Pasco said again.

Otto was standing now, finding it hard to believe he was still alive. Grim-faced, he slipped his buckle and the belt and gun fell to the ground. His brief moment of panic had left him. He had faced death but death had not come. "You'll never get another chance like this, Pasco," he sneered. "Why don't you go ahead and kill me—or have you lost your guts?"

Nothing he could say could bother Pasco now. A great weight had been taken from his shoulders. For the first time in five years, he felt free. "Call it that if you want to," he said quietly, still backing away from his horse. "But I wouldn't bet on it, if I were you."

Otto was undecided. He glanced at the gun lying at his feet, wondering if he could somehow reach it and fire before Pasco could pull the trigger.

"You can't do it, Otto," Pasco answered his unspoken question.

Otto laughed harshly. "You've lost your guts, Pasco!" But he wasn't sure enough of it to make a play for his gun. "There'll be another time, Pasco."

"Maybe."

The word was hardly out when he saw something happen to Otto's face. At first, Pasco thought Otto was going to throw himself at his gun, but then he saw the rancher go sprawling in the opposite direction. Otto yelled—one word, a senseless word that meant nothing—and instinctively Pasco wheeled, moved one step toward Keller. At the same instant he had heard the ear-splitting crack of a rifle, and a bullet burned through the spot where he had been standing.

Pasco hit the ground—hit and rolled and scrambled for what protection he could find, exactly as Otto was doing. The rifle barked again, and this time the bullet kicked up dirt in Pasco's face and went screaming toward the far end of the creek. There was no time to think, but Pasco knew that the firing was coming from the other side of the watering hole. At the same time he remembered the noise he had heard earlier in that direction—but he had no chance to wonder about it now. He thought wryly: It looks like I owe Otto an apology about the bushwhacking!

Otto grunted, his fat red face a puzzled picture of anger.

"It's my backshooter, it looks like," Pasco said.

"The dirty son!" Otto had clawed his way to the edge of the pool, and on the way he had picked up his gun. He fired once, twice, three times, as fast as he could pull the trigger. Pasco fired once and then moved on all fours to the scanty cover of a salt cedar. Keller's anger seemed to have changed directions again. Now he was venting his spleen at the unseen rifleman across the pool.

Without looking at Otto, Pasco said, "Did you see who it was?"

The rancher spat. "All I saw was the glint of sun on the rifle barrel. That was enough."

They lay still for a moment, the uneasy silence still shaken by the explosions of their guns. "There he is!" Otto hissed, and at the same moment Pasco glimpsed the dappled figure of a man darting through the brush on the other side of the pool. Each of them fired once, but the figure had disappeared before they had pulled the triggers.

"He's heading downstream," Pasco said. "I'm going after him."

Otto hesitated for just an instant, his eyes darting from Pasco to the gun in his hand. He spat again—whatever had been in his mind was discarded. "Make no mistake about it," he said. "I hate your guts, Pasco. But even more than that, I hate a jasper that shoots from behind. I'm dealing myself in."

At that moment it seemed only natural that they should throw together to stop the bushwhacker. Even now they could hear the rifleman thrashing about in the tall weeds, far down the creek.

"He's probably got a horse down there," Pasco said. "If we're going to stop him, we'll have to hurry."

Half crouched, they left their cover and began crashing through the undergrowth. At the lower end of the pool they paused to listen and reload their revolvers. Silence settled over the creek again.

"He's making a stand somewhere," Keller said. "Probably he'll be waiting for us around the bend."

Pasco grunted, punched out his empties and inserted fresh cartridges into the chambers of his .45. And all the time he was wondering why anybody but Otto would want to kill him. The bushwhacker would have had to kill Otto too, for he couldn't have a witness to the shooting.

There was no answer now, although a vague, uneasy idea was beginning to form in Pasco's mind.

"One of us will have to cross the creek," Otto grunted. "Then we'll be able to box him in at the bend—if that's where he's making his stand."

Without a word, Pasco eased down the bank of the creek and waded across. On the other side, he motioned to Keller, and both men began moving along the edges of the creek, their guns ready.

Up ahead Pasco saw the bend—one of the sharp hairpin turns that gave Crazy Creek its name. Suddenly the rifle blasted again, echoing and re-echoing as the noise ricocheted from one creek bank to another. The bullet ripped wildly into the brush and slammed into the trunk of a cottonwood.

Pasco went down to one knee, the hammer of his revolver making two metallic clicks as he pulled it back. But there was nothing to shoot at—not yet. After a moment he began moving forward again, Pasco catching glimpses of Keller on the other side of the creek as the heavy man lunged from one bush to another. The rifleman opened up again, this time in Otto's direction.

Pasco saw Otto stumble and go down, but he had no way of knowing whether he had been hit or if he had tripped himself in the undergrowth. At the same time the rifleman came out from behind the protection of the clay bank, shooting at Pasco with a .30-30 repeater.

For a split second Pasco stood in dumb surprise, as the killer showed himself. Then he hit the ground, rolling out of the deadly rain of lead. What happened next was not clear to Pasco, and never would be, for he had no wish to remember it. Somehow his .45 was still in his hand. He felt it buck as the rifleman charged crazily toward him up the sheer clay wall.

The rifleman stopped suddenly, then lunged back as though he had taken the impact of a sledge in his stomach. He fell near the edge of the water, struggled for one brief moment to get up, and then lay still.

The killer was Marshal Bunt Wallace, and Pasco knew he was dead. . . .

After the thunder of violence, an almost unbearable quiet settled over the creek bed. Pasco stared dumbly down at the fallen marshal, feeling sick and tired and a thousand years old. He had already guessed that the rifleman had to be Bunt Wallace. The shooting at the wagon yard, and again on the creek the night before—both times the marshal had been too close to the scene. But—

Wearily, Pasco holstered his revolver and crossed the creek again. He thrashed through the brush above the creek bed until he reached the place where Otto Keller had fallen.

The fat rancher lay doubled on the ground, clutching at a spreading circle of red on his shirt front. Pasco knelt beside him. The last words Keller said, were, "Tell Myra . . ."

"Tell Myra what?"

Otto's eyes rolled up and stared unblinkingly at

the blazing sun, and after a moment Pasco closed the rancher's eyes and stood up. Otto Keller was dead. He had died thinking of Myra. Whether or not he had been cursing her, Pasco didn't know. He didn't want to think about it.

There was no hate left in him, and no anger. He was ready to drop from exhaustion. At last he turned and walked woodenly down to the edge of the water where Bunt Wallace lay.

What did I ever do to you, Wallace? Why were you so determined to kill me?

The marshal would never answer. He lay face down in the sand. Cool, clear water lapped gently over the toes of his boots. Somebody will have to be notified, Pasco thought stupidly; and somebody will have to tell Myra.

He didn't dare ride toward the Rocker-O headquarters. One of Otto's men would kill him before he had time to explain. The best thing would be to head back toward Hornsby's range and tell Doc Fuller and Peg. They'd know what to do.

At last Pasco bent down and began dragging the marshal's body away from the water. Sweat broke out on Pasco's forehead and dripped into his eyes as he set doggedly about the job.

Then suddenly the answer became clear. Wallace himself had solved the riddle, after all. As Pasco tugged at the body, the marshal's hickory shirt rode up his back. The pale, dead skin of

Bunt Wallace's back bore the mark of the whip.

Quickly, Pasco turned the dead marshal over and studied his face. The whip marks had nudged the missing piece of the puzzle into place—and now Pasco knew where he had seen the marshal before.

Perhaps a minute passed, or an hour, as Pasco stood staring down at that face. It was almost as though he were looking in a mirror and seeing himself for the first time. Myself, as I might have been, he thought. The sweat on his forehead was cold.

Very gently, Pasco untied the marshal's neckerchief and spread it over the face, and then he started heavily downstream to where his horse was picketed.

"John!" The voice startled him.

Pasco snapped erect, and then he saw her perhaps a hundred yards upstream, coming toward him from the direction of the water hole. It was Myra.

Pasco's first impulse was to get away from her, but his feet didn't seem to want to move. He stood woodenly, watching her fight her way through the brush.

"John! John, you're all right!" Her voice was choked. Pasco shook his head slowly, in amazement, and a startling thought came to him: *poor Otto!*

She glanced quickly at the marshal's sprawling body, then away. Sobbing, she flung herself at Pasco, and clung to him. Pasco stood like stone, unfeeling. Why don't you ask about your husband, Myra? he thought.

"It's over!" she said tightly. "Oh, John, it's over!"

"Yes. Otto's dead," Pasco said flatly, "if that's what you want to know, Myra. I didn't kill him. Bunt Wallace did."

She stared at him, uncomprehending.

Pasco had no idea why he bothered to go into details. Perhaps, he thought, I have to convince myself that it's really happened. He said, "I intended to kill Otto, but something happened. Something you wouldn't understand."

She continued to stare at him. And, for some reason, Pasco went on. "It's a long story," he said, almost to himself. "Wallace tried twice before this to kill me—and I didn't know why until a few minutes ago. A while ago he tried to kill both of us. Wallace must have trailed me to this place last night or this morning, but Otto showed up before he could get a clean shot at me. As far as Wallace was concerned, that meant that Otto had to die too."

She still couldn't believe it, and Pasco couldn't blame her for that. It was still incredible to him. He started to go on, but he knew instinctively that he could never make Myra understand, and he wasn't sure that it would be worth the trouble to try. Then Myra looked at him, her eyes bright.

"John, it's ours, now! It's all ours!"

He merely stared.

"The Rocker-O—don't you understand? And the Double-O Star. And Hornsby's Crazy Creek, too, before long!"

Pasco felt a bleakness. He said hoarsely, "Good-by, Myra." Turning quickly, he broke away from her and hurried through the brush toward the lower end of the stream.

If Myra called to him, Pasco didn't hear. When he reached his horse, he climbed wearily into the saddle. He pointed the animal toward Hornsby's range. Whether it was too late to change, he didn't know. How can a man tear down in a few minutes what it took five years to build?

He can't—not alone.

He began to understand why he was headed again toward the Crazy Creek.

Chapter Fourteen

The silence, the uneasy air of a false peace still hung over the ranch buildings as Pasco rode through the open gate toward the headquarters house. Then he saw Peg Manning standing in the doorway of the barn—the building now serving as a temporary hospital—and he reined his horse in her direction.

"Well!" Silas Hornsby stepped out of a saddle shed and came toward him. "I expected you'd be back, Pasco," he said. "Maybe I'm a fool for doing it, but I kept your job open for you. Hell's about to break loose up at the Forks. You'd better get up there as soon as the wrangler can cut out a fresh horse for you."

Pasco had almost forgotten about the range war. It would be easy enough now to take over the Forks and dam off the Rocker-O water supply. But he knew that Hornsby would lose in the long run. He wasn't fighting Otto now, or old Hilderbrand—he was fighting a woman who was set on power, and there was nothing she wouldn't do to get it.

Pasco wanted no part of it. Completely dulled with fatigue, he climbed down from the saddle. The feeling of lightness was in his head again, and he thought: God, I hope I don't act the fool and faint again! Not until I can talk to Peg, anyway.

Hornsby said, "Where're you going?"

"I want to ask Peg about something."

Silas frowned. A doubt was beginning to gnaw at him—but he forced it back and said with forced heartiness, "Well, I'll have your horse tended to, and get a fresh one cut out for you."

Pasco walked over to the barn where Peg was standing. He glanced over and saw four riders on straw pallets, covered with blankets. There would be more, he thought, before Myra achieved her end.

He said, "Can we walk off a little way, Peg? I've—got something I want to tell you." She gazed at him steadily, and at last she nodded. Pasco walked beside her to the empty corral behind the barn, and then to cover his nervousness, he fished for the makings of a cigarette. But his hands were unsteady, and he threw the crumpled paper away and put the tobacco back in his pocket.

He said, "Otto's dead."

Her eyes went wide. It wasn't the way he had meant to start, but he guessed it was as good as any. Peg hadn't said a word. All she had to say was in her eyes—weariness, and defeat, and disappointment. Then Pasco said, "But I didn't do it, Peg. It was Bunt Wallace."

She didn't show the surprise that Pasco had

expected. She merely closed her eyes for a moment, and when she opened them again something about her had changed.

"I had the chance," he said, and he wasn't sure why it was so important that she should know this. "But at the last minute I changed my mind," he went on doggedly. "I don't think I could tell you why. There are some things, I guess, that can't be put in words."

Not looking at him, she nodded. "I think I understand."

"I had to kill Wallace, though. There was no other way."

And then he told her what had happened on the creek; about all of it except Myra. He didn't want to think about Myra.

He explained about the marshal.

Still Peg didn't seem very surprised. "Maybe it was my fault for not warning you," she said heavily. "I didn't know it was Wallace, of course, but I knew there was something about him—something wrong. He tried too hard to be a good marshal. It was an obsession with him, and he only succeeded in making people hate him. And we never knew where he came from."

And Pasco said, "Ever since I first saw him, I had the feeling that I'd seen him before somewhere. But it didn't occur to me until it was too late."

"The prison?" Peg had already guessed.

Pasco nodded. "I knew when I saw the whip marks on his back. I have marks just like them." Suddenly he shook his head, as though he were trying to dislodge the thought from his mind. "I think I know why he did the things he did—why he tried to kill me. But I don't know if I can put it into words."

"Try," Peg Manning said quietly. "Maybe it will help, John."

He said, "To explain what Wallace did, I'll have to explain myself. Are you sure you want to hear it?"

She smiled the smallest smile in the world. "Yes, but it's more important that you hear it."

Her words made no sense to Pasco, but after a moment he went on. "I've never told anybody how it was when they let me out of prison, and I'm not sure that I can. Killing Otto Keller was all I could think of—even though I knew it would be the end of everything. For a while I tried to lock it up in my mind and forget it. But it wouldn't work. Every time I got a job somebody would find out about the marks on my back, about my prison record, and they'd let me go. A man can stand just so much of that, and then something in his mind breaks, like a boil bursting, and the poison spreads through him. He reaches the point where he can't force himself to ask for another job, because he knows beforehand how it will end. That is when he begins thinking there is only one solution—a gun."

Peg was staring at him curiously. "And you think that is the way it was with Bunt Wallace?"

"I'm sure of it. Probably he had lost as many jobs as I had, maybe more. Then one day he came to Messina and they gave him this job as town marshal. At last he was somebody. People looked at him with a kind of respect. And he took pride in doing his job well—too well, possibly."

Peg Manning said, "Then you came to Messina and he recognized you. Sooner or later, he knew, you'd recognize him and expose him."

"I wouldn't have."

"But that was what he thought. He believed that killing you was the only way he could hold onto his security in Messina. Is that it?"

Pasco nodded. "I guess so. His record would have come out sooner or later, no matter what he did with me. But he couldn't see that, I guess— just as I couldn't see it for a long time."

"Do you see it now, John?" Peg looked at him steadily.

Pasco hesitated. "I used to wonder," he said finally, "about ex-convicts that came back to their old jobs and were accepted as if nothing had happened. I've even heard them joke about it, and I used to wonder how their bosses trusted them. Now I know it was because they weren't trying to hide anything—the way I was, and the way Wallace was."

Peg waited a long while before she said, "What are you going to do now, John?"

He hadn't thought about that, but he knew there was only one thing to do. "I'll leave Messina," he said. "There's nothing here for me—" and then he added bluntly—"except you, Peg."

For the first time, she looked away from him.

She said finally, "And then what, John?"

". . . I guess I'll have to start all over again. Maybe it won't work. Maybe nothing was ever meant to work and I'll keep running up against a rock wall. I'll have to have help, Peg. I mean—"

She looked at him then. "I'll wait for you, John. Is that what you want?"

She said it quietly and decisively, as though she had already thought it out in her mind. Pasco reached for words to tell her it was exactly what he wanted, but the words were not there. "I guess I've been a fool, Peg."

"We won't talk about it. That part is over now."

Pasco half heard the sound of spurs as Silas Hornsby came toward them. The rancher was beaming. "We got him back with us, Peg. I figured he wouldn't stay away long."

Pasco turned. "I'm not staying, Silas."

"What?" The rancher's face was red.

Then Pasco said, "Otto's dead," and he watched

the color drain from Hornsby's face, as the rancher stared in disbelief.

"Dead!" Hornsby tasted the words, seeing himself as the new boss of the Panhandle.

You'll never make it, Hornsby, Pasco thought without emotion. By the time you get around to following up, Myra will have recruited a new army.

"Otto Keller dead!" Silas lingered over the thought. "You'll get everything I promised—the ranch and all that goes with it."

Pasco had forgotten all about the promise, and now the thought left a taste of bitterness on his tongue. He said shortly, "Forget it, Silas. I didn't earn it."

The rancher's eyes popped. "I tell you—" But Pasco didn't listen. For just a moment he took Peg Manning's hands in his.

"You're going now?" she asked.

He nodded. "I'll go into Messina and tell the sheriff what happened. Then I don't know exactly where I'll go. But I'll be back, Peg."

"I know you will."

"As soon as I find work, I'll come back for you, Peg," Pasco was saying.

Hornsby turned abruptly, and walked angrily toward the cook shack. The damned fool! he thought. He could work as my foreman, or he could have a ranch of his own!

Then the rancher stopped and stared out at

the sprawling prairie—the monotonous grassy sea flowing out in all directions. All mine! he thought. I'll own it soon. Of course there's no need to hurry now, if Otto's dead. There's just a woman now to stand in my way. I'll take my time. Silas Hornsby smiled to himself.

His mind occupied with the thought, he didn't see Pasco standing in the doorway of the barn, holding Peg Manning in his arms. He couldn't see the doom gathering over the prairie like a summer thunderhead. And he couldn't see Myra, in a headquarters building, venting her rage and frustration on the hapless Rocker-O riders, waiting impatiently for her new army to arrive.

At the sound of hoofs, Hornsby turned and saw Pasco riding out of the ranch yard, headed toward Messina. The rider looked back and lifted a hand, and Peg Manning waved back.

The fool! Silas Hornsby thought again. What can he expect from the future? The best he can hope for, to start with, is an ordinary cowhand's job. Later, maybe he can get on as foreman somewhere, or maybe he can stake out on a barbed-wire outfit of his own and starve a little more every year until he gets to be an old man. And maybe he'll marry Peg Manning and they'll raise more kids than they can feed. And to think that he could have married Myra Hilderbrand!

Silas called to the wrangler to cut a horse for him. He thought he'd ride up to the Forks and tell his men to take it easy for a while. From here on out things would be easy.

Above, the invisible thunderheads rolled silently. Silas Hornsby paid no attention.

Center Point Large Print
600 Brooks Road / PO Box 1
Thorndike, ME 04986-0001 USA

(207) 568-3717

US & Canada:
1 800 929-9108
www.centerpointlargeprint.com